*Encounter
Christ
Through the
Dramatic
Story of*

vinegar boy

Encounter Christ Through the Dramatic Story of

vinegar boy

ALBERTA HAWSE

MOODY PRESS
CHICAGO

@ 1970 by
ALBERTA HAWSE
Moody Trade Paperback Edition, 1989, 2002

All Scripture quotations are from the King James Version.

ISBN: 0-8024-6588-9

1 3 5 7 9 10 8 6 4 2

Printed in the United States of America

Dedicated to my grandchildren:
Debra, Tamar, Carl James, and Alberta
And to my great-grandchildren:
Aaron, Robert, Beth Ann, Ryan, and Andrew

CONTENTS

PART 1

THE DAY OF SADNESS

1
THE ERRAND

Light began to flow from the jug of the morning. Horns at the holy Temple on Mount Moriah lifted their long throats and welcomed the sun with silvery blasts. The first rays splashed on the window ledge of the high attic room and slipped under the sagging shutters to form golden puddles at the feet of the sleeping boy.

In the towers of the Fortress Antonia, looming over the room where the boy slept, a sentry walked to an open balcony and, putting his hands to his mouth, announced a change of guard.

The boy awoke with a start and, thrusting back his blanket with his feet, stretched his toes toward the trickling sunbeams. He smiled as his toes communicated the promise of a beautiful day. Then, turning on the pallet, he held out his hands to the golden beams. They filled the hard brown palms and spilled down his wrists. Dust particles danced in the golden stream, and he laughed as he snatched at them.

His laughter bubbled from within with the singing gladness of fine wine rushing from the tap. The same bubbling gladness filled him as filled the vats in the commissary cellars far below.

Today was *his* day to do with as he willed.

There would be no work in either vegetable garden or hop fields, no errands to run for the fortress, because Nicolaus, the commissary steward, had promised him that today would belong to him.

"You deserve it," the steward had said, blinking his pale blue eyes to keep out the tears, as the boy confessed his desire. "You deserve His favor, boy, and He will know it, for it seems He knows the hearts of men. I wish I could go with you to find Him, but the armorer has my promise to help with his inventory."

It had not been easy to confide in Nicolaus, either, though they loved one another as a father and a son loved. The hope had developed slowly. His heart had cradled it as the nest of his friend the sparrow would cradle its speckled eggs. And it had only been this week, as the Temple shook with the voices of the multitudes, that the hope had cracked the shell and thrust forth to articulate speech.

"I am going to ask Him to heal me," he said, and Nicolaus, who had been pouring the milk for him, stopped and laid his hand on his shoulder. That was all, but he knew that the steward's blue eyes would be filled with tears, even as his own were swimming, and he did not raise his head to see.

But he had been glad when Nicolaus said he could not go with him to find the Nazarene on the great porch of the Temple. The joy would be too great for either of them—they were both soft of heart. No, it was better for Nicolaus not to be there. But when it was done he would come back, and Nicolaus would put his hands on his face and turn him this way and that, and his voice would rise—booming big and rough and ragged—and he would probably wipe his nose on his big apron.

The boy laughed as he thought of it. He rolled over on the blankets; then he jumped to his feet and lifted a simple hop-hemp garment from the peg by the window. He yanked it down over his straight red brown hair and his clean, tanned body. Twisting a length of rope about his waist, he thrust his feet into the pair of boots Nicolaus had cut down for him. He pulled the straps together and laced them with the thongs. Nicolaus had told him it would be best to reserve the boots for another summer, but the steward would not care if he wore them to the Temple today.

His legs looked thin in the calf-high boots—thin as the sparrow's. He flung open the shutters and looked up toward the eaves where the new nest had been built. The sparrow, waiting for him, fluttered down with a chirping welcome. The boy leaned out to smile at the waking world.

His eyes shone like amber wine, and the rays of brightness struck red from his hair. But in the glow of the sun, as his face lifted, the left cheek remained blotched and darkened as if the dregs of a heavy purple juice had stained it.

The sparrow settled with a rustling of wings on the worn slab of the sill. He cocked an apologetic eye as the boy began to scold.

"Sparrow! Did I not tell you to waken me early? Have I not told you what great and marvelous thing will be done for me this day?"

The bird flicked an embarrassed tail.

"You still expect me to feed you?"

The answer was a decisive chirp.

"If I failed to do what Nicolaus asked me to do, would I be fed?"

The sparrow bobbed its head, and the boy laughed. He reached for a small bag of grain on the shelf by the window. "You're right." He poured a palmful of the grain on the window ledge. "Nicolaus would feed me no matter what. He is soft of head and heart, Nicolaus is. But tomorrow, if you do not waken me in time to get to the hop fields early, there will be no morning rations. Today I have to forgive you. I cannot allow the smallest weevil of ill-will in this day's omer."

The sparrow chirped, fluffing his feathers, and some of the grain drifted down into the sunless area of the barracks' ground below them.

"Even you will not know me tonight," the boy said, shaking his finger at the bird. "Not even you, my undependable friend. And after the mark is gone they will not call me names again. None of them can call me names again." The boy's eyes went out to the bulky shadow of the Roman barracks. "The new ones will have no reason to inquire of the boy with the liver face."

The glow had left his eyes, and there was a slight edge to his laughter. "And Phineas—ha, my good friend Phineas. How angry he will be, Sparrow. When the butcher sees what the Nazarene has done for me, his eyes will pop out like those of his own dead fish."

The amber eyes began to sparkle again. "When you have finished with the grain, Sparrow, you must fly out toward Bethany and find Jesus for me." He pointed. He could not see, but he knew it well, the road to Bethany that led away beyond the eastern gates, up the slopes of the mount where the silver gray olive trees dotted the hillside, and out of sight over the hill where Bethany lay at a crossroads. And the Man who stayed with friends in Bethany would be on His way to Jerusalem.

"Go, Sparrow, and find Him. He has come in on the Bethany road each day this week. I could not leave the hop fields to speak to Him, for the plants are tender and weak as your birdlings will be when they break the shell. If you wish to be forgiven for not waking me, you must find Him. Tell Him that Vinegar Boy of Jerusalem is coming to seek a favor. Tell Him it is a very little favor, Sparrow, for One who can do so much."

The last of the grain dust drifted off the sill. The sparrow spiraled upward into the sunlight and passed over the barracks and the foremost towers. The boy watched him out of sight and then put the bag of grain on the shelf and closed the shutters.

He was folding the blankets of his bed when Nicolaus called from the foot of the narrow stone stairway.

"Get up, boy, the trumpets have blown." The steward's hearty voice brought a smile. Nicolaus too had been warned to waken him early.

"I'm coming." He ran down the steps. The hobnails in his boots struck happy sparks in the dark stairway. Nicolaus was at the foot of the stairs, blocking what light came from the wide doorway beyond.

"I'm sorry I had to waken you, but—"

"I was awake—talking to Sparrow. I've sent him out to Bethany to tell Jesus that I am coming. I want to be among the first to greet Him on Solomon's Porch."

Nicolaus moved back, and the boy caught sight of his face.

"What is it, Nicolaus?"

"I'm sorry, boy. Your trip to the porch will have to come later. There is an errand for you. I just got an order from the fort."

"But Nicolaus . . . you promised!"

The boy stopped. He knew the man well enough to know that if Nicolaus was breaking a promise it was something he had to do. Something that Nicolaus could not help, so he might as well not cry about it.

He tried to hide his disappointment as he stepped from the stairs into the wide hallway where doors led into various workrooms of the commissary. At the rear of the hall a ramp led downward into a labyrinth of cellars and storerooms that wound like monstrous entrails beneath the hulking height of the Roman stronghold.

"I'm sorry," Nicolaus repeated. "I meant for you to have the whole day. But I've just asked Phineas to bring up the vinegar when he fetches his own rations for the day."

Vinegar! The boy's heart dropped. When Nicolaus said it like that it meant just one thing. A crucifixion. Vinegar laden with a drug called myrrh was given to the condemned men to ease the pain.

He could feel himself go pale and knew that the blotched cheek must be standing out in extra ugliness. "No," he whispered. And then, "Who?"

"Their names I do not know, but I had orders to fill a bottle for three. The fellow who brought the order didn't know much. He said he thought two of them were from the rebels in the dungeons. One of them broke a guard's arm last night as he passed the food to him. But there seems to be an element of mystery about the third man."

"Would it be Barabbas?" Barabbas was the most notorious prisoner in the cells. A leader of a band of marauders who ravaged the Roman caravans, he had gathered about him a band of rebels and zealots who had never surrendered to the dominion of Rome when the land fell under the control of the Caesars.

"Marconius is in charge."

The boy knew that Nicolaus was trying to lighten his disappointment. Centurion Marconius was a good friend.

"I wish I could send someone else, boy, but as long as the tribune considers you garrison property . . ."

The boy understood. Nicolaus had raised him as a son from the time a patrol had brought him in from the hills where he had been abandoned, but Nicolaus had not adopted him legally. Not that he was not willing, but the boy himself, since he had been old enough to understand, had not agreed. Nicolaus was too good—too honorable—to be burdened with a birth-marked son. If a boy's own mother and father could not stand the sight of him, why should the steward be afflicted with him?

But in the past weeks, as the hopes for a miracle had slowly developed in the boy's breast, they had discussed the adoption at great length. The boy would pick a name—a real name—and then they would go before a judge and have all things done legally and in order.

"When you are my son you will never be sent to the hill again." The boy knew that Nicolaus had been talking to him as his mind wandered.

"It is all right, Nicolaus. I will hurry. But if the Romans have to kill their enemies, I wish they could find a better way to do it. Nobody is mean enough to die on a cross."

Phineas, the butcher, stepped from the cellar ramp, carrying a flaring torch in one hand. He thrust it into a jar of dirty water to quench it, and the odor filled the hall. Then he hung the torch on the wall by the cellar entrance. In the other hand he swung a flagon of vinegar on a leather strap and carried a pitcher of wine for his own use.

His green eyes glittered as he came near. "Why should you worry about the rebels? The quicker they are cleaned out, the better for the rest of us. What have they done with their protesting except turn the fury of Rome against peaceful people?"

Phineas had evidently heard what he had said to Nicolaus. It seemed to the boy that Phineas always knew what he and Nicolaus said to one another. The butcher seemed to have ears that could turn corners and climb walls.

Nicolaus answered for the boy. "Death is no less death if it comes swiftly and with mercy."

Phineas laid back his lips in an ugly grin as he thrust the bottle of drugged wine at the boy. "The two of you make a good pair. One is about as chicken-hearted as the other. You feel sorry for the rebels, but you give not a thought to the Romans who are left in the hills with their throats cut."

The steward's voice rose, round and rolling as one of his own beer kegs. "I do not condone murder and thievery, Phineas, but I understand a man's right to fight for his own freedom."

"Freedom!" The butcher spat the word. "Who wants freedom? I am eating twice as often and three times as well since the Romans came. And you—what is so precious about your freedom, Steward? You wear your freedman's cap as if it were the crown of Herod. But I am more free than you because I have not cared for freedom. With meat for the stomach and wine for the bowels, what else can a man desire?" Phineas lifted his wine pitcher and laughed. His big yellow teeth and the odor of the myrrh rising from the vinegar bottle made the boy half ill. The liquid in the leather flagon squirmed under his hand. The mouth was stoppered with a plug of wood wrapped in an oiled cloth. He slipped the strap of the bottle over his shoulder.

"You are a reprobate, Phineas," Nicolaus said. "Somewhere at some time you were put through a press that squeezed all the compassion out of you."

"Because I think thieves should earn their own bread? If the rebels enjoy slitting throats, let them not squawk when their own throats are threatened."

The boy put his hand on the bottle. "There are three men, Phineas. Did you put in enough wine for three?"

"I put in what was ordered and not a drop more."

Nicolaus said, "There is enough, boy."

"And the myrrh?"

"I put the drug in the bottle myself."

The smell of the myrrh was still rising, and the boy pushed the stopper in tighter. The drug would help the pain, and later, as the men were tormented with thirst, a sponge would be soaked in the sour wine and lifted for them to suck on.

"I need a sponge," he reminded Nicolaus.

Phineas growled, "There are some old ones by the draining trough in the slaughter shed."

The thought of the blood-heavy sponges, the flies, and the odor made the boy's stomach turn. Nicolaus gave the butcher a warning look.

"Don't let him worry you, son. You'll have a clean sponge."

The butcher brushed past the boy on his way to the wall where the day's requirements for meat and poultry were posted. As he went, he spoke under his breath. "Get out of my way, Liver Face."

Vinegar Boy had not realized that Nicolaus had

ears as sharp as the butcher's. But Nicolaus had heard him, and his blue eyes blazed with anger under the bushy brows. His short body with its heavy shoulders, and fists that could crack the head of a cask with one blow, moved swiftly behind Phineas, His hand swung the butcher about, and the big fist gathered up garment and flesh indiscriminately.

"Phineas, I am telling you for the last time. As long as I am steward of this commissary these rooms are my own household. In my house this boy is to be treated as my son. Is that clear?"

His voice did not rise, but the knuckles of his hand were white. The butcher's face burned with anger, but fear leaped in his green eyes.

"The boy is going to have a name one of these days, but until such time you call him nothing but Boy, as I do." Nicolaus shook the butcher now—side to side, front to back. The butcher bleated weakly, and Nicolaus released him. He did not see the malevolent question that Phineas's eyes cast at the boy. But Vinegar Boy saw and read it as plainly as if Phineas had scrawled it on the wall.

What decent name can a bastard child have?

The look demanded an answer. "When I come back tonight I will have a good face. Then I will have a name—a name just as good as anybody's."

Phineas rolled back his lips. "So I have heard." The heavy door leading to the butchering sheds slammed behind him. The boy turned to the wide doorway leading to the yard. Nicolaus followed. The bricks of the barracks' ground were covered with a fine layer of dust that muffled the sound of his boots. Beyond the barracks, the gates opened to a large parade area where the troops held daily practice in defense formations, archery, and sword and spear skills as well as ordinary bodybuilding exercises.

Nicolaus laid a hand against the boy's cheek. "If He does not come to the Temple today, you may go as far as Bethany. Do not fear to ask the favor of Him. You are a good boy and deserve a good thing. He will know it. When it is done, tell Him that I, Nicolaus the freedman, stand ready to become His friend."

The steward's broad Gallic face was serious, his blue eyes grave.

"If for any reason you must keep the cheek as it is, we will still go before the judge. Marconius will arrange things for us as quickly as we give the word."

The boy's amber eyes warmed, but there was no smile on his face. "I am not afraid to ask Him, sir. He does not hold back His skirts as the Pharisees do. He will see my need, and He will know that I must have a new face." Then he said, "Get me the sponge right away, will you, Nicolaus? I must come back quickly, for Sparrow may have told Him already that I am coming."

"If I have to open a new crate it will take a few minutes. Why don't you eat while you are waiting?"

Vinegar Boy shook his head. Eating could wait. It didn't pay for him to go to the hill with a full stomach.

2
WHAT NAME?

Vinegar Boy waited impatiently on the bench outside the commissary door. If Nicolaus had to open a new crate of sponges, he would count each one and check the total against the shipping manifest. Nicolaus never did anything in a hurry or by guess. Not so much as a handful of animal salt left the storerooms without an accounting. He would take time to jot down the entries concerning the amount of vinegar drawn for the execution detail. He would record the sponge and the weight of the myrrh.

Sometimes Vinegar Boy believed that Nicolaus revered honesty as much as freedom. In fact, Nicolaus had often said that a thief and liar knew nothing of freedom, regardless of what their manumission papers said. Nicolaus cherished his documents of freedom and kept them in a strong box in a chest in his sleeping quarters. The small freedman's cap with its conical top scarcely left his head while he worked. And he never set foot outside the fortress without it.

Nicolaus knew about slavery and freedom and understood the desire of the revolutionaries to be free of the Roman oppression—to drive them from their beloved Galilean plains and Judean hills. He did not approve of the outlaws' murdering and stealing, but he understood their hunger to be free. Although he did not condemn the rebels for being willing to fight for freedom, he himself had won the precious possession in an entirely different way.

Nicolaus had been a slave. He was a Gaul, the grandson of a Gallic soldier who had fought under the leadership of the mighty Vercingetorix. The wild, longhaired Gauls fought hard to preserve their land from the hordes of Roman legions invading it from the south. Vercingetorix and some of his men, after many days of ruthless siege, had been taken by Julius Caesar. They were carried with other spoils of war into Rome, where they were loaded with chains and paraded in degradation during a victory celebration for Caesar. After the parade they were tortured and killed.

When Nicolaus told Vinegar Boy about it, he said, "My father was just about your age when they forced him to watch his own father being torn apart by four horsemen. From that moment on he hated the Romans with a hatred that was like a consuming disease."

As they had talked that night, Nicolaus had poured the evening milk and divided the cheese while the boy warmed dates in oil in a pan over the fire.

Then Nicolaus went to the heavy chest in the corner of his room and took out a parcel of old clothing. He spread the apparel over the end of the table: a short pair of work-worn trousers and a Gallic cap that had a peak almost like a freedman's cap.

"These belonged to my father," Nicolaus said as he

lifted the garments gently. "The Romans laughed at his trousers and his cap. They called his dress barbarian, though they were glad enough to adopt the trousers for their own winter wear. They laughed at his long yellow hair—the pride of the Gauls. But my father never ceased to wear the trousers or the long hair. He wore them in rebellion. He was a slave, but he never surrendered to the Romans. He wanted me to hate them as he did, but I could not. The man who bought me was a kind man—a young patrician who later became an army officer. I had no reason to hate him. My desire to be free was strong—as is all men's—but I could not hate a good man. My father never understood."

Vinegar Boy spooned out the portions of fried dates. "If you had hated him you would not be free now, would you?"

Nicolaus shook his big, bald head. "No. And worse, I might have murder on my conscience."

Nicolaus had won his freedom as a gift from the Roman who owned him. They had been traveling in the mountains of Galatia during a light snowstorm. The Roman's horse slipped, and horse and rider toppled over the cliff out of sight. Nicolaus heard the plummeting horse hit with a thud far below. But close at hand he caught the wind-whipped cries of the Roman. He crawled to the edge of the mountain trail and saw the Roman swinging over space, his hands clutching an outcropping rock. One stomp of Nicolaus's boots on the Roman's hands would have crushed the fingers and sent the dangling form into the chasm below. Or he could have walked away from the man, who was begging for help. No one would ever know that the horse had not carried his rider with him to the rocks below.

But Nicolaus had not stomped or turned away in the rising blizzard. He made a long, strong loop with his cloak and, swinging it beneath the dangling feet of the helpless Roman, he pulled him to safety. The Roman had taken Nicolaus before a judge and given him his freedom papers as an act of gratitude.

While Vinegar Boy had been thinking of the cold mountain cliff and the old clothing that Nicolaus had shown him, the day had begun in earnest at the barracks. Squawks from the fowl pens told him that Phineas was making the selections for the day. Commissary servants and slaves scuttled about the yard, carrying kindling and coke for the fires to be built beneath the scalding tubs where the meat would be dipped and dressed.

The doors of the barracks opened behind the high arches of the colonnades, and the men came out, stretching and yawning in the fresh air. They called ribald jests to one another and to the sentries on the balconies and in the towers above them. Some of the jests made the boy's ears burn. Nicolaus had taught him to avoid the rude and the vulgar, to hate the ugly word or nasty deed. He tried to shut his mind against the rough language as he had tried to learn to shut out the hateful remarks and curious glances concerning his cheek.

He moved his boots restlessly and wished he had gone to the warehouse with Nicolaus. Usually the steward let him count the sponges in the new crates. The lid would snap open, and the sponges would leap out and roll on the floor as if they were alive.

Marconius, his centurion friend, had told him that a Greek scholar named Aristotle had decided that sponges *were* alive—that they were little animals. Vinegar Boy accused Marconius of teasing him because sponges were not like animals at all. They had no ribs, no backbones, no skin.

But he had since learned to believe all things that the Roman centurion said, and now he did believe that sponges lived and breathed on the floor of the ocean. Men's lungs were like the sponges, Marconius had explained. The air squeezed in and out, and the air kept men alive. When breathing stopped, life stopped.

Vinegar Boy shivered. The butcher had explained it in his own cruel way. Phineas had grabbed him one day and slapped his greasy hands over his mouth and nose. He couldn't breathe, and terror and panic filled him. His head swelled, and his chest hurt. When Phineas released him, he stumbled into the open air, gasping and incoherent.

He had learned about asphyxiation that day. He knew then why the Romans considered the death thrust of the spear during a crucifixion an act of mercy. For the death thrust was used only on the crucified men whose leg bones had been broken and who could no longer lift themselves to fill their lungs with air.

Today there would be the breaking of legs and the death thrust for those who were to die—for the rebels and the third man, whoever he might be. No bodies would hang outside the gates of Jerusalem over a holy holiday, and today was the preparation for the most important Jewish feast—the feast of the Passover.

Vinegar Boy swung the flagon of myrrh and sour wine slowly between his knees, thinking again of the day Phineas had grabbed him and suffocated him with his slimy hands. Sickness rose in him as he thought of it. He had never told Nicolaus what Phineas had done. The steward would have given the butcher a lasting taste of his own medicine.

The boy had learned a long time before that Phineas could be trusted to do the mean and hurtful thing at all times. It was Phineas who had told him the truth about himself. Not that Nicolaus had ever tried to keep the truth from him, but from the steward the truth did not hurt.

One day, almost eleven years before, the soldiers had found a discarded baby in the hills. They had carried him into the garrison as a joke, for one cheek was fair and the other a hideous purple-red, as if he had lain too long near hot coals.

The soldiers joked about the child being sired by Janus, the two-faced Roman god that often appeared over doorways and temples. The god's smiling visage was meant for good, and his scowling countenance meant war or misfortune.

When the novelty of the birthmark had worn off, the soldiers left the baby with Nicolaus and told him to dispose of him in any way he wished.

Nicolaus had kept him. He told the boy later that he could not resist the beauty of his amber eyes and the red-brown hair, like the shining back of the barley beetle. He had made a bed from blankets and a broken-down vinegar cask. From then on, as the men of the garrison inquired about the child, they began to speak of him as the vinegar boy. New recruits would come to see his face and go away exulting in their own good fortune.

The boy had never thought it such a terrible thing to be a *found* baby when Nicolaus told him about it, for the steward made it sound as if he considered him a gift from the gods.

But when Phineas explained it, his abandonment in the hills became a thing of dreadful shame.

"No wonder your mother gave you up and your father refused to accept you. Who could stand such a face day in and day out?"

Sitting on the bench now, tears filled the boy's eyes. Smoke from the scalding tubs ascended the slaughter-pen walls and drifted into the barracks' grounds to smart his eyes. He rubbed at them and thought of the day Phineas had said those awful things to him. He had crawled behind a bin of turnips, hoping to die.

Nicolaus had found him and gathered him into his big arms. The steward had smelled of sweat and beer that day, and the boy found comfort in the odors. Later, Nicolaus talked with him.

"You cannot go through life with a heart like an unwalled city, boy. You must accept yourself for what you are—a fine lad. I could love you no more if you had proceeded from my own loins and had a face as flawless as Apollo's."

Vinegar Boy turned his back to the smoke and blinked the burning from his eyes. Why was he thinking about such sad things?

Today was not a day for sadness. Today was *his* day—a day of gladness. Always, like weevils in the grain, a day had a portion of ugliness and labor and sorrow, but today he must remember that happiness would be measured to him in abundant portion.

He would ask his favor of the Nazarene, and then he would pick a name.

He leaned his head against the dried-brick wall of the commissary and closed his eyes against the growing brightness of the day. He could smell wet feathers and the scalded flesh of the fowls. The servants and slaves chattered like magpies on the balconies of the barracks and in the courts, as well as on the marble porches of Pilate's fortress-palace quarters. In the courts, the servants sounded like a gaggle of geese.

What name could he choose when he didn't know if he was Roman, Greek, or Jew? Had his mother wanted to call him David? That was a royal Hebrew name because it was the name of a mighty king. Or perhaps his father had decided on Julius or Augustus. But these the boy did not like. He wanted no Roman name. Perhaps he was Greek. Nicolaus often told him that he had the questioning mind of a Greek. He might call himself Timotheus or Philip.

Which would it be? Or did it matter? Even with a name and a good face, would he not continue to carry the shame of being dropped on a mule trail in the hills?

Would not the butcher, even then, be able to whisper the ugly name that meant he had sprung illegally from his father's loins—unwanted and undesired, fit only to be purged away as the wild runners were pruned from the hop plants in the fields?

3
EVIL
LAUGHTER

As Vinegar Boy stepped out of the garrison into the deserted street, the heavy door of the depot thudded shut behind him. The sponge, tied with the rope at his waist, bobbed lightly on his left hip. The vinegar bottle on its thong hung over his right shoulder.

Outside the fortress walls he turned to descend sharply into a narrow, high-walled canyon in which the morning mists were settled like waters in the stagnant sea.

In the few years he had been running errands for the garrison he had learned the city well. He knew all the quickest routes to the city gates. He knew which garden walls could be scaled, which rooftops could be crossed. He was familiar with old and abandoned alleys.

Today his path led downward through one of the ugliest and dirtiest of the tenement districts and then northward through the lavish Roman baths and gymnasiums to the Damascus Gate. He would pass along the old Jewish markets, cross the line of the ancient walls, and go through the old gates into the avenue that led to the new Roman market. Some of the civic buildings were of white and rose-misted marble that glowed like warm flesh. Across the portals, brilliant frescoes gleamed; and on the porches, the colorful mosaic tiles made the boy think of runaway flower gardens.

Statues of gods and humans, sadly mixed in the Roman mind, according to Nicolaus, guarded the portals of every building and lined streets and highways. Nicolaus often said that the Romans had a god for every day in the week, the month, and the year. Scarcely a month went by that they did not hold a festival in honor of some important deity. But the more Rome pressed her many gods upon the consciousness of the Hebrews, the more the Jews reiterated their ageless commandments. "I am the Lord thy God, which have brought thee out of the land of Egypt, out of the house of bondage. Thou shalt have no other gods before me. Thou shalt not make unto thee any graven image. . . . Thou shalt not bow down thyself to them, nor serve them: for I the Lord thy God am a jealous God."

Today and tomorrow the Jews would celebrate their release from the land of Egypt. The story would be retold in every home—how the angel of death, sent from the Lord, had swooped low over every house in the land of Egypt, gathering to himself the firstborn of every generation of both man and beast, from the son in the deepest dungeon to the servant in the furthermost chamber of the palace.

Only those homes where the blood of a lamb had been sprinkled escaped the sudden slaughter.

In the quiet of the misty street, Vinegar Boy's boots clicked with a lonesome sound. He wondered how he would feel if he were a Jew celebrating a feast of freedom from Pharaoh while he was under bondage to Caesar, who was worse than Pharaoh. Caesar Tiberius of Rome ruled Judea, and he was revered not only as emperor but also as god.

In Jerusalem, Pontius Pilate, as governor of Judea, spoke for Tiberius and for Rome. Vinegar Boy tried to imagine what had happened in Pilate's official quarters at the fortress during the night as the trial was held and the death order given. No one could send a man to death except Pontius Pilate.

Why had it been done so swiftly and so secretly? Certainly everyone in the city and surrounding countryside knew that the rebels would be ordered to the hill sooner or later. But they had been in the dungeons under the Fortress Antonia for a month. There had been no talk of an execution—certainly not on this day, a Jewish holiday. It was not the custom, and Pilate tried to keep peace in religious matters.

The third man must hold the key to the mystery. Who could it be?

One thing sure, he thought. *It can't be Barabbas. He is too important to be destroyed secretly. They'll use him for a horrible example as to what can happen to a man who speaks treason or rebellion against Rome. They'll take him to Caesarea, or even to Rome, where he will have to fight the wild beasts—or be given a choice of some equally awful way to die.*

No, the third man was probably not Barabbas. Whoever it was must be important. But who could equal Barabbas as an enemy of Rome? No one!

Vinegar Boy remembered the night the patrol had brought in the small camp of rebels. The moon had been white and full—heavy as a ewe with lamb. For weeks the seditionists had been especially violent, as Roman patrols had been ambushed without mercy.

Caravans, intended for the palace and the fortress, had been stripped. Caravan leaders were slain and camels and donkeys slaughtered as a lesson to others who might be persuaded to haul for Rome.

The city had been plastered with placards offering rewards for information leading to the apprehension of Barabbas, the rebel chief. Tiberius had sent couriers from Rome with word that this insurrectionist had to be stopped!

Every man at the fort had been alerted. The patrols were tripled in number, and they had combed the hills with fine teeth. One day they had found a rebel camp, and those who were not killed in the onslaught were dragged behind horses into the garrison.

Barabbas was among those captured. Advance word had come to the garrison, and the patrol was met with a midnight revel.

The boy did not like to remember all that he had heard or seen from his window that night, for the things that had been said and done mocked the purity and gentleness of the swollen moon.

The moon had been full again last night as the boy and Nicolaus and Centurion Marconius sat on the bench by the commissary door.

They had spoken of another Man as different from Barabbas as the sun was different from the moon. Jesus of Nazareth was a Man of gentleness. The rumors concerning Him had started as a gentle rain the first of the week. Winds carried the gossip from Galilee and Samaria and from Perea beyond the Jordan River.

Then suddenly the gentle rain had changed into a storm. Rumors swept like backwash into the corners of the barracks, bearing accusations and condemnations from the religious leaders in Jerusalem.

"Arrest this Man. He speaks against the Temple."

"Stone Him. He works the work of Satan in Jehovah's name."

"Cast Him out of the synagogues. He made Himself one with God."

But over the stormy abuse, others could be heard giving praise. Mothers held out their stricken children for the hands of the Nazarene to touch; blind men crawled to Him to receive sight; sick men, placed at His feet, rose to join the chorus of acclamation.

"Behold Him! Our Messiah!"

"Lift up your head, O Jerusalem, for your deliverance draweth nigh."

"Hosannah to the Son of David. Blessed is He who cometh in the name of the Lord."

The abuse and the praise mingled until even the soldiers of Rome climbed to the topmost balconies of the Fortress Antonia to watch the people in the Temple courts below as they pressed about the Man called Jesus.

As the three of them talked on the bench under the white light of the moon, Nicolaus asked Marconius why his men had not arrested the Nazarene. The priests and the scribes had howled for His arrest on the charge of teaching blasphemy and error. Notices for His arrest and offers of rewards for knowledge of His whereabouts hung side by side with the posters advertising the hunt for Barabbas.

Marconius tipped his head back against the bricks. "Rome has no legitimate quarrel with this Man. The placards are Pilate's balm for the Jewish leaders. Their skin is being rubbed raw by the Nazarene. Once or twice I have had to send my men to disperse a crowd. The first of this week there was a veritable triumphal march from Bethany to Jerusalem. But many who laid their garments before Him and waved palm branches were but exuberant children."

Nicolaus clasped his hands over his thick stomach. They rose and fell in heavy rhythm. "He preaches freedom and equality. Is that not a threat to Rome?"

Marconius ran his hands through his short dark hair, which Vinegar Boy had always thought was black as the inside of a bunghole. "His lieutenants are fishermen. I doubt if any of them has ever swung anything more deadly than a scaling knife."

Vinegar Boy laughed.

Nicolaus raised wise blue eyes beneath the brows that still held a few stiff yellow hairs. "He is *good,* my friend. Goodness and liberty will conquer all emperors eventually. Your Caesar gives his legion the sword, but this Nazarene arms His disciples with love."

The boy listened closely. Nicolaus was very wise and almost always right.

"Maybe you and I will not live to see the day, centurion, but love will win. Men will be free, for they were created to be so."

Marconius shook his head and smiled. "What is there to fear in a Man restoring another man's hearing when at the same time He advises that man to obey authority? He declares that it is the meek who shall inherit the earth."

Nicolaus stirred abruptly. "Is that not what I have just said? Wherein is meekness if it is not in love?"

Marconius conceded the point reluctantly, but there was more he wished to say. "If He were to seek recruits through His miracles, we would fear Him, as we have feared the popular appeal of Barabbas. But Jesus calls no one to rebellion. Quite the contrary—" The centurion's voice softened. He leaned forward. In the moonlight the sweat line of his helmet was like a scar across his forehead. "He calls them to rest—as a weary people tired of sacrifices and labor. He calls them to rest. 'Come unto Me, all ye that labor and are heavy laden, and I will give you rest,' He says. He offers a permanent peace in a world that has no peace. No, Steward, I see no cause to *fear* this Man, but I can understand why men *follow* Him."

Nicolaus stretched his heavy arms across the boy's lap and laid his hand on the Roman's knee. "I would not suggest your shouting your sympathy aloud from Pilate's porch."

"Have no fear. I know that what I say to you and the boy in confidence will go no further."

Now, as his hobnails rang on the cobblestones, Vinegar Boy felt again the surge of warm pride that he was included in the centurion's trust.

Ahead of him on the street there was a small intersection where the cart wheels had worn deep ruts in the pavement stones. He paused on the curb to catch his breath, for he had been walking fast. The smell of hot ovens and browning loaves came from behind a high wall that flanked one corner of the street. He could hear the groaning whines of the flour mill, and the delicious odors made his mouth water. He took a deep breath of the baking bread and stepped down. A stone rolled under his foot, and his ankle turned sharply. The pain went quickly but the bottle of vinegar had begun to gurgle noisily. There was something about the muffled sound that reminded him of Phineas and his evil laughter.

He put his hand on the side of the bottle and said sharply, "Stop it." But the wine continued to swirl and gurgle, and suddenly the boy felt chilled, *The wine knows something about today that I do not know*, he said to himself. And then he shivered.

4
MAN UNDER
THE STAIRS

As the city awoke, the tenement blocks began to hum. The narrow windows in the ancient, plastered walls always reminded the boy of the combs of wild honey to be found in the hills.

During the day, the children clambered over the windows and through the doorways, much as the wild bees went in and out of the comb.

As Vinegar Boy passed the last of the waking tenements, he came into the area of small Jewish shops. The sidewalk tables were empty, the awnings tied down, the shutters closed and locked. Near a vegetable stall he saw fat, gray rats gnawing on a pile of old cabbages that had been dumped at the curb. Clenching his hands, he held himself to a steady stride, trying to make himself heavier so his boots would sound louder on the pavement. A few of the rats scurried behind a sewer grating, but several stood their ground. He could feel their malignant stares on his ankles as he passed. He was thankful for the calf-high boots. When the sickening smell of the rotting vegetables was behind him, he found his palms wet with sweat.

A little later, he passed beneath the high-arched colonnades of the avenue of the wigmakers and the beauty shops. Sometimes the shops had wigs on display. Many of them were made from the bright yellow hair that came from the women in the land of the Gauls. Strong yellow hair, such as Nicolaus once had.

Near the beauty shops, the Roman baths sprawled in splendor. Wide marble porches and porticoes provided a place to gossip or transact business. Romans loved their public baths with the pools of hot and cold running water and the steam chambers, but the Jews scorned the baths, for they did not believe in the public exposure of human nakedness.

Beyond the beautiful wide avenue of the baths and gymnasiums, Vinegar Boy entered a dismal street that ended at the front of two decrepit apartment buildings. Between the crumbling buildings an old stairway led downward through darkness and filth to a closed alley. On the lower level, new shops had been attached to the back of the old building. The new shops faced the square, and their new walls extended across the alley area with only a narrow space left open between them. Most people had forgotten, or never knew, that behind the walls the old stone steps could still be used to get to the street above.

The stairway was rotten and dangerous. The planks of the steps had been grooved and laid across square pegs sunk into the walls of the apartment buildings on either side. Slops and garbage were sometimes tossed from the sunless windows of the tenement walls above. In some places the planks had rotted and splintered and fallen into the dark well be-

hind the steps. Where the planks were missing, anyone climbing or descending the stairs had to use the
supporting pegs as a ladder—trusting themselves to
the pegs' insecure grip in the crumbling mortar.

As Vinegar Boy left the street and started down the
steps, cold, fetid air swept upward about him. He had
never told Nicolaus about the old stairs for he knew
the steward would not let him use them, and they
were the quickest route to the immense square inside
the north gate.

As the stinking air swirled around him, he tried to
hold his breath. He went slowly, feeling his way with
hands and feet. His palms pressed hard against the sides
of each building. The new boots did not cling to the
steps or the pegs as well as his sandals. Once a chunk of
plaster slipped from beneath his hand and crashed in
the darkness below him. The sudden movement of the
plaster caused him to slip, and he grabbed frantically at
the wall. The step beneath him turned, and one boot slid
off into space. He crouched, grabbing for the steps behind him. His heart thumped, and its beat made an
echo in his head. The vinegar bottle hit the wall with a
thud, and the vinegar splashed angrily.

He didn't move for a little while as he tried to gather courage. Then he stretched his leg, and his boot hit
a solid step. Slowly he stood upright again. Below him
he thought he heard a rustling sound. Remembering
the rats that lived in the dim shadows behind the
steps, he felt his panic returning.

If he could get to the bottom safely this time, and
out into the clean sunlight, he would never use the
stairs again. If he fell and cracked his head on the
stone stanchions that held the last few steps, Nicolaus
would never find him. The rats would have his flesh
before he was cold.

He began to descend again, breathing easier after each step. The building on his right did not extend as far toward the walls of the false fronts of the new shops facing the square as the building on his left side. Three bottom steps had no right-hand wall into which to anchor the wooden pegs. Here the planks had been laid solidly on columns of piled cobblestones. As he reached this section of the stairs, he drew a relieved breath. A glow of pride warmed him. Once again he had come down the dangerous stairway victoriously.

He stood quietly for a moment, wiping the gritted plaster from his hands on his garment. Then he stepped down. One more step and he could cross the area of deepest shadows and reach the bright opening in the walls where a narrow shaft of sunlight slipped in from the square.

He tried to adjust his sight to the darkness. As he stood, pressing the sponge at his waist with a nervous hand, he felt himself grow tense. He had stretched one foot for the last step but now he drew it back. He held his breath and listened. There was a strange odor in the alley—an odor of danger.

He heard breathing. The flesh of his neck began to crawl. Someone was in the alley with him. Whoever it was must be waiting in the well of blackness behind the stone columns of the steps. Beyond the strip of sunlight in the front walls he heard the traffic of the square. If he could reach the walls he would be safe. He would have to make a run for it!

He gathered his strength and jumped. Hitting the dirt floor of the alley, he would have plunged ahead if his boots had not slipped on the damp and rotten earth. He tried to run, but a hand caught his arm and almost jerked him off his feet. Big fingers, strong as an iron trap, settled into his shoulder muscles and held him captive. A voice, hoarse and urgent, spoke behind him. "Help me, boy."

At first Vinegar Boy could not make out the man who held him. But as his eyes became accustomed to the small amount of light that fell through the broken steps, he saw that the man was big and hairy. He wore nothing but a loincloth, and his chest and arms were matted with blood. The odor of blood hung in the alley.

"Help me," the man said again. And though the fingers still pinched him in pain, the boy saw that the man was weaving with weakness.

"What do you want me to do, sir?"

The man tried to answer, but his shoulders sagged, his fingers lost their grip, and he fell forward slowly. His knees buckled, then his body straightened, and he fell face forward with his hands outstretched.

Vinegar Boy knelt beside him and looked closely at the wounds. From the nape of his neck to his ankles there was not a handbreadth of flesh that had not been flayed by the scourge. The boy put his hands under the heavy shoulders and heaved the body over. The face, rough with beard stubble, had been smashed with iron knuckles. Lips were broken and eyelids torn.

He lifted the heavy head on one arm and used his teeth to pull the plug from the bottle of drugged wine. Then he poured a thin stream of the vinegar into the lax mouth. The man swallowed, then choked. His eyelids fluttered. "Water," he muttered. "Fetch me some water."

The boy stoppered the bottle and let the flask fall to his hip.

"Can you sit up, sir?"

The scourged man groaned and struggled. Vinegar

43

Boy pulled, and finally the beaten body was propped against the frame of an old doorway that had once opened into a small oil cellar beneath the stairs.

"My stomach is on fire, boy. Get me some water."

Vinegar Boy straightened up. He could feel his garment sticking to his knees. His hands were bloody too. The man's fingers, hairy as hop vines, closed again about his arm. "Get me some water—water!" The battered eyes seemed hard and evil in the sparse beams of light.

"I can't if you don't let go of me. There's a fountain in the square—"

"You promise you'll come back?"

"Yes—if you let me go so I can quit wasting time."

"Swear by your mother."

"I haven't got a mother." The fingers were hurting him, and anger began to replace fear. "See, I will leave the bottle with you as a pledge." He swung the vinegar from his shoulder with his free hand.

The man swore softly under his breath. "That stinking stuff? What is it?"

"It's for a crucifixion. It's got myrrh in it."

The man drew a deep breath. His hairy hand reached for the bottle. "Wine for the hill, is it?" He began to chuckle.

At first the boy did not recognize the obscene sound as laughter. The chuckles convulsed the man's chest and made the muscles of his thick neck quiver. "Wine for the rebels? And I am the first to taste it? Strange indeed are Jehovah's ways."

5
THE
THIRD MAN

He was still shivering as he slipped from the alley and stood in the sunlight with his eyes closed against the glare on white marble and pavements. The sun was warm on his eyelids. He could hear the sounds of the main entry of the city about him. Small carts rumbled through the gates. People were coming and going, chattering in holiday mood. Over the noise of the traffic he heard the splashing of the fountain across the square. The smell of the cold water carried to him on the morning air.

The fountain had been built many years before by Herod the Great. A smiling bronze mermaid rode the back of a marble dolphin. Both mermaid and dolphin had grown a little worn about the edges, and the mermaid had lost the fingers of one hand. But the water that fell about them from the aqueduct pipes was clear and cold.

The overflow of the fountain basin ran into a series of troughs. Vinegar Boy leaned over the horse trough and tried to wash the blood from his arms and his garment. He rubbed the spots furiously. If he failed to get the stains out, he would have to explain to Nicolaus about the alley and the dangerous stairs.

A few frowzy-haired women with sleep-laden eyes filled their water pots at the pipes. Suddenly their chatter ceased, and the boy knew why at the moment the silence fell. His cheek began to flame. Shame and hurt pushed his breath into a lump in his throat, and he was angry with himself for caring. He had heard that sudden drop of conversation before—that sharp intake of breath, half horror, half pity—and then the thin, excited whispers. He bent his head quickly and began to splash the cold water over his face. The heat in his face died, but the anger continued to lie like a hot, heavy coal in the middle of him.

The women resumed their chatter, set their water pots on their shoulders, and moved away.

Vinegar Boy went to the line of public gourds sitting on the fountain rim. He selected a fair-sized one —about the shape of a man's head—and waited his turn at the pipes. Water from his garment dripped down his legs and into his boots. He could feel the water oozing lightly about his toes. His boots had begun to rub on toes and heels. He was proud of them, and glad he had worn them, but they were stiff. They would be hot and heavy before the day was over. But even heavy boots would not keep him from sprouting wings after he had seen the Man from Bethany.

Even now Jesus might be coming in the eastern gate. And surely Sparrow had been faithful to deliver his message to the Nazarene. He must get to the hill and back as quickly as he could.

Then, standing with the crowd on Solomon's Porch, he would not push or demand to be first; he didn't care if he was the very last. But he would not leave the court until Jesus had granted the favor. So easily and so quickly Jesus would remove the ugly color. As easily as a man could use his hand to erase writing in the sand, just so easily could Jesus take the mark away.

The slap of a driver's hand on the rump of a donkey brought the boy out of his reverie. A trader had come into the city with a load of Cypriot kettles. Vinegar Boy admired them though they were covered with dust. The man's brows were thick with dust, also, and his black eyes burned from lack of sleep. He bent his head beside the donkey and slopped water over his face.

When he stood up, flipping the water from his fingers, he motioned outward toward the hill.

"Something going on today?"

"Yes, sir. A crucifixion."

"They can't let the crosses rest, even on a holiday. I saw some people going up—thought it might be a stoning."

Vinegar Boy shook his head. The place of the Hebrew executions was near the mount. People sometimes stood on the southern edge of the cliff to cast the larger boulders, but the boy had never seen a Hebrew stoning. The Jewish laws were strict and merciless in their own way.

"Who're the unfortunate wretches?"

"Rebels, sir. Two from the camp they captured last month. Another man is going to die, too, but I don't know who."

"We heard they got the old hawk himself. Any truth in it?"

The driver meant Barabbas. "Yes, sir, they did."

"Maybe he's your third one."

47

"I don't think so, sir. I live at the garrison, and we heard that the governor might send him to Rome in time for the emperor's birthday."

"You mean for the gladiatorial games?"

"Yes, sir."

"Heathens!" The trader clacked his tongue, and the boy noticed that a tooth was gone from the front of his mouth. "Are you going out?"

"Yes, sir, I *have* to go."

"Sure, everybody has to go. What is there about a thing like that to draw people like gnats?" He clacked again. "Leeches! That's what they are. Blood-hungry leeches!"

"But I *do* have to go, sir, I—"

"Oh, sure." The driver gave the donkey a slap. "A boy like you ought to tend to his own business." And the donkey moved away, the brass kettles bobbing and swaying.

Vinegar Boy watched him go, and he could feel exasperation rising. Did that man think he *wanted* to see a crucifixion? Some people thought they knew everything.

He turned back to the pipes and filled the gourd to the brim. Behind him, as he crossed the square holding the gourd carefully, he heard the sound of marching feet. There was no mistaking the sound. Once, he had marched with the death procession. He heard the heavy tread of the boots, the sound of the horses' hoofs, and, farther away, the sound of mourners.

Usually women and children did not accompany the condemned men to the hill. Once in a while a father or a son would be allowed to go with the condemned man, but women were almost always turned back at the north gate. If they wanted to see the crucifixion, they had to follow at a great distance, or climb the hill by themselves.

Vinegar Boy stepped out of the street and onto the sidewalk. He held the cold gourd against his chest and waited. Now that the scourged man had delayed him, he would let Marconius and the soldiers go ahead of him.

Ever since he had gone to the hill with the condemned man, he had avoided the slow and horrible journey. As he waited for Marconius and the prisoners to come into sight, he thought of that first journey to the hill. Nicolaus had hesitated about sending him on the errand with the vinegar, for he was not yet eight years old, but the tribune at the fort had practically commanded the steward to assign the duty to the boy. "He really belongs to the garrison, doesn't he? He has to earn his keep some way," he said.

Nicolaus had spoken to the tribune almost as an equal. The boy already earned his food and more, he replied. He worked in the vegetable gardens that had been assigned to the fort; he was learning to work in the hop fields that supplied the fortress brewery.

But the tribune had insisted, not unkindly, "The boy has to grow up, Steward. I have sons of my own. I know how you feel about the boy. I would like to protect my sons from the harder things of life, but I cannot. Send him out. He needs to know that there is more to living than can be found behind the safety of the fortress walls and the stone fences of the gardens."

So Nicolaus had tried to prepare him for that first errand with the vinegar. He tried hard, and when he had begun to speak of good and evil in terms that the boy knew, it had gone well. "Seeds of wickedness and goodness grow side by side in the hearts of men, my son. Remember that this is so in your own heart as well as in the hearts of others. Nurture the good. When the leaf of wickedness appears, pluck it out as you have learned to rid the fields of that which will strangle the good crops. Insofar as you are able, let only the good seed flourish."

Now, in the sunlight with the cold gourd chilling his chest, Vinegar Boy heard the sound of weeping and remembered that first trip to the hill. There had been but one prisoner. A murderer. A man who had killed a Roman citizen in a dispute over the promised price of a pair of hand-carved cedar chests.

A woman and a small girl had followed the man from the prison gates through the streets that day. The little girl had run beside her father, sobbing, "Why are they hurting you? Why are they hurting you?"

She carried a doll made of polished olive wood, whose features resembled her own. And at the gate, when it came time to turn them back, the child screamed, and the mother clung to her husband's legs.

The guards had to pry them loose and use their whips to drive them away. When they were gone, the boy saw the girl's doll in the dust. He would have picked it up, but the father stumbled and fell under his beam, and the whips cracked. When he rose, the doll was not to be seen in the cloud of rising dust.

Later, on the hill, when the man was disrobed, the doll fell out of his garments. He pleaded for it, but a soldier grabbed it, broke it in half, and slung the pieces over the face of the cliff.

Then the victim had broken down and begun to sob, pleading for his life so he could care for the child and her mother. The boy had grown sick at his stomach.

He had told Nicolaus about the girl and her doll and the screaming man. That night he woke with nightmares.

Nicolaus had told him that he must never go with

the death march again. "Go early. Leave the vinegar in the old shed." This the boy had done. But sometimes there were other errands to run for the officers or the men on the hill, and he had learned to close his ears and eyes to the ugliness. But his stomach always betrayed him.

The gourd of water grew heavy and colder. The traffic cleared slowly from the center of the square as the standard bearer came out of the sunless street. His white horse stepped in time to the beat of the lone drummer. He held the Roman insignia aloft with solemnity and arrogance.

Behind him, Centurion Marconius rode on his gray stallion, Rubicon. The brushlike plume of his helmet curved like a blackbird's wing over his head and down his neck. His cloak was a blotch of scarlet in the street.

Marconius seemed troubled and preoccupied. He looked neither to the right nor left as he rode, and Vinegar Boy could not catch his eye.

Behind Marconius, the young Syrian officer Arno walked. He was smaller than the centurion, and his helmet and breastplate were of leather and brass.

Each of the condemned men carried his own wooden crossbeam over his shoulders.

Four guards from the Fortress Antonia accompanied each prisoner—one in front, one on either side, and one behind. The soldiers on the side toward Vinegar Boy carried the whips.

The boy found himself waiting anxiously for a glimpse of the condemned men. The first rebel was a heavy-chested giant with a gray beard and a partially healed sword slash on his left ribs.

The second rebel was young. His cheeks bore a short stubble of straw-colored beard, but his hair was a mass of golden curls. As he came into the sunlight, he lifted his face, and the boy could see strange ecstasy upon it. He seemed to be drinking in the sunlight. Surely this one was a worshiper of the sun.

But neither of these men could be Barabbas.

Neither could the third man be the famous outlaw, for he was surrounded by weeping women, and few women would be weeping for Barabbas. No sympathizer would be foolish enough to arouse Rome's suspicions by showing concern for the chief rebel of the hills—the hawk of vengeance, as many called him.

Vinegar Boy stepped from the sidewalk and tried to get nearer to the man who was bent almost double under the weight of his beam. He was evidently not as strong as the hill men. His sandal strap had broken and seemed to trip him now and then as he moved along. His garments showed stains about the shoulders, and the boy wondered if he had been whipped. It was unusual for scourged men to be crucified.

The scourging generally preceded release—a warning for the man to mend his ways.

A thought flashed across his mind. The man in the alley had been scourged. He must be a freed man. Then why was he hiding in fear of his life?

People were coming into the square from all streets now, and Vinegar Boy was pushed aside. The standard bearer had reached the gates, and men in the gate towers blew their trumpets to clear the portals and let the procession through.

In the center of the square, the weaving column came to an abrupt halt as the man with the broken sandal strap stopped. He stopped so suddenly that the soldiers fell out of step. In the momentary confusion, his voice was raised, "O daughters of Jerusalem—"

At the sound of his voice, the women fell to their

knees. Some even went prostrate on the pavement, and the boy got a full look at the third man. The sun fell in a blaze of white on his face. He had been beaten and battered almost as much as the man in the alley. Portions of his beard had been yanked out. Patches of raw, bloody flesh flowed purple and red—worse than the mark that burned on the boy's cheek. The bruised lips opened, and the neck of the crossbeam carrier strained upward. "O women of Jerusalem, weep not for me, but weep for yourselves, and for your children. For if they do this while I am yet with thee, what will they do when I am no longer at hand?"

The whip rose. The man staggered on. The women fell back slowly. A very few, not more than three or four, followed at a distance when the procession left the gates. Those who turned back helped bear one other up.

The gourd had driven a chill right through to Vinegar Boy's shoulder blades. Where had he heard that voice before? "Weep not for me." Something flopped and quivered inside him. He stopped one of the weeping women and asked, "Who is he? That man who spoke to you?"

The woman stared from dull dyes. "Begone," she said. "Leave us to mourn in peace."

But her companion gazed on the boy with reddened eyes. "Did you not know him?" she asked. "The Rabbi of Nazareth?"

The fire of the birthmark flamed on the boy's cheek. The gourd dropped from his hands. Water splashed his boots, and the woman brushed the drops from her dusty skirts as she went on, lost in her misery.

Vinegar Boy looked after her with dazed eyes.

Jesus of Nazareth was going to die? Why? What

had He done? If they killed Him there would be no more miracles—

He started to run—to follow the procession—but his boots kicked the gourd, and it spun in the sunlight, holding him in a grip as strong as hairy fingers.

The memory of his promise turned bitter on his tongue. He had told the man he would be back; he had left the vinegar as a pledge. Jesus would need the vinegar.

The boy cast a frantic look northward. Already the crowd at the gates had obliterated the death procession.

He grabbed the gourd from the pavement stone and dashed for the fountain again.

6
THE
HIDING HOLE

When Vinegar Boy returned to the alley, the man was still crouching on the worn sandstone sill of the old cellar doorway. Two weather-beaten boards had been bolted across the doorframe to keep the worm-eaten planks of the door from falling into the alley. The hinges were of cracked leather, and as the man leaned against the door, the whole frame moved under his weight. The bolts that had been used to fasten the supports were loose in the walls.

Vinegar Boy held the gourd for the man. As he drank in huge, painful gulps, impatience pounded in the boy's veins. *Hurry! Hurry!* he screamed to himself.

The man's life depended upon the water, and he drank as if he were fully aware of it. When he finished drinking, he told the boy to pour the rest of it over his bare, raw shoulders.

"Easy—it burns like hot iron."

The water ran slowly between the channels of open skin and matted hair, carrying blood and bits of flesh with it. A puddle formed in the hollow of the sill beneath the man. And when at last the gourd was empty, the man said, "Now I will have another swallow of wine."

The boy held it out reluctantly. The vinegar flask looked small in the man's hand.

"Not too much, sir. And please—I have to hurry. I have to get to the hill. The procession has already left the city."

The big hand cracked the stopper so hard that the boy feared the neck of the bottle would burst. "I heard them. Tell me, was there one with short hair—like an ember?"

"Yes, sir. He seemed glad to be in the sun."

"How is it today? The sun?"

"Strong and climbing fast."

"Good. Dysmas was afraid they would take his head off in the dungeon. He wanted to die in the sun —if he had to die." The man's fist began a low thudding on the old doorframe. He began to curse low and violently. The boy waited.

"Is Dysmas your friend?"

"As close to me as any man could be, not of my loins. The Romans took his father's vineyard years ago—over his father's body. And the boy has been in the hills with me ever since. Together we gathered a Roman neck for every grapevine they had stolen."

The hatred in the voice made the boy sick. A silence fell, and he held out his hand for the vinegar. "Please, sir, I have to go." And then he frightened himself, for he heard himself asking, "You are a rebel, sir?"

One did not go about Jerusalem asking men if they were rebels.

The man ignored his outstretched hand. "I am a

zealot. I want nothing for our nation except what belongs to her. Through the promises of Abraham and
Moses, this land is ours!" Again his fist brought hollow echoes from the depths behind the door.

"Why did they beat you so hard, sir?"

The man looked up, and Vinegar Boy caught a
gleam of shrewdness and honesty in the outlaw's eyes.
"They hate me more than any other man. And what I
have tried to figure out—all these hours in this stinking hole—is not why they beat me but why they set me
free. 'You can go,' they said, and they dragged me out
before the night watch ended. And when I asked why,
they growled like jackals deprived of a kill. 'The
priests have brought in a bigger bird,' they said."

His words hung labored and heavy in the murky air.
"When they finished with their fists and their whips,
they hauled me out to the gate and threw me down."

Air whistled in painful gusts from the flayed chest.

"They expected me to leave the city. Pilate sent
word that they were to release me. But I knew they
were waiting; in the first gully they would have had
my heart. They have no intention of letting me get
back to the hills. But I will! I will!" Again the heavy fist
echoed. "I told them the old hawk would not die. No,
not before their cursed legions take their screaming
eagle back to Rome."

The effort of talking took strength, and the violence of his hatred weighted his speech. Then the
hand that had struck the doorframe shot forward and
gripped Vinegar Boy's thigh. "How well do you know
the city?"

The big fingers gripped a muscle, and the pain
made breathing difficult.

"I know it well enough. I have run errands for the
garrison for three years."

"The underground passages? The caves and the sewers and the old tunnels—do you know them?" The boy nodded. "Well enough to get me outside the city without taking me through a main gate?"

"Yes, sir, I think so."

"You *think* so?"

"I know I can. But not now. I haven't time to do anything more for you right now. I have to get to the hill." He stopped suddenly. How could he stand here arguing with this man when Jesus was about to die? Who was this man whom Pilate had chosen to save rather than Jesus of Nazareth, who had done nothing but good? He had to know.

"Sir, who are you?"

The answer came short and swift. The boy could not believe that he had heard it rightly.

"Barabbas? The outlaw leader? I don't believe it. Pilate would never release you. Never in a million years. Tiberius would kill him!"

"But he did, boy, and he sent a Man named Jesus to the cross." There was a change in the heavy voice. An uneasiness pervaded the words, as if he had been asking himself a question for hours and the answer still eluded him. "I wish I knew why; Rome could have no greater enemy than Barabbas."

"Jesus wasn't anybody's enemy!"

On the upper street level, near the entrance to the old stairway, children could be heard laughing and shouting. One threw a rock down the ancient stairwell; it struck the steps and bounced over the boy's head. He heard it strike the soft earth behind him.

"Jesus brought people back from the dead. He didn't *kill* them."

"I have heard that they accused Him of being one

with us. But, as you say, boy, from the little I knew of Him there was no likeness between us."

"He helped people. He did miracles. He—" Suddenly Vinegar Boy made a desperate decision. He had to go. Leaning forward, he grabbed at the vinegar bottle in the outlaw's hand. Barabbas, startled by the onslaught, brought his arm up quickly. His elbow caught the boy on the chest and sent him reeling backward. His head cracked against the edge of the stone columns.

The pain made stars, and through the whistling blackness he thought he could hear the man saying, "I'm sorry. Here, let me—" Barabbas was standing, trying to probe his head for a cut. And the boy, even while his head reeled, could not get away from the sickening odor of blood and sweat. His stomach churned.

"L-l-let go of me," he stammered. "Let go."

Barabbas was still holding him, leaning forward slightly. A shaft of light fell for a moment full on the boy's face, and the man gasped. "What's the matter with your face, boy? I sure didn't—"

His head was clearing. The stars had converged into the dim light of the alley. "You didn't hurt my face. It's a mark. A birthmark—since I was born."

Barabbas clucked. The sound, so unexpected, made the boy think of Nicolaus. He could feel the rush of hot tears to his eyes. His head ached, and his stomach was still turning.

"I was going to get it fixed today. Jesus was going to fix it—"

" And so He could, boy. I don't blame you for wanting to be rid of it." There was comfort in the words, and they tore down the dam of restraint. The boy's words came with the tears. "This was supposed to be *my* day, and it's spoiled. They should be killing *you* instead of Him and—" Barabbas said nothing and the boy babbled on, telling of his need, of his desire for a name, and how Nicolaus wanted to adopt him.

When the boy was finished, feeling childish and foolish and ashamed, the outlaw said softly, "I understand. And I want you to have your miracle."

He put the bottle of vinegar into the small, trembling hands.

"Go—while there is still time."

Vinegar Boy gripped the bottle, and his heart lifted in thanksgiving. "But—what about you, sir? If they come in here and find you, they might—"

"They won't find me."

"Will you hide until I get back? I'll come back and take you out." Another idea came springing. "Or I could draw you a map, sir. If you think you could make it on your own."

Vinegar Boy slipped the strap of the bottle over his shoulder and searched for a piece of plaster. Then he moved to the boards that covered the old door. "Now listen and watch closely." He sounded like Nicolaus giving instructions. "Here there is an old sewer grating that can be lifted. You must go back up the stairs, and here the old tunnel connects with the cistern. From there you turn left into the corridors that lead behind the old stables—" The map drawing went on until the line came out beyond the pool of Siloam in the southeastern corner of the lower city near the valley of rubble where a man could make his way to the Salt Sea and into the mountain ranges of the wilderness of Moab.

Barabbas listened. He leaned forward to study the map through his swollen lids. His breath came hard, and bubbles of blood formed on his beaten shoulders. Vinegar Boy threw the chalk down.

"It's no use. You couldn't get through by yourself. You'd come out in the wrong place and get killed."

"You're right," Barabbas agreed. "I couldn't make it, boy. Not by myself. But I have an idea. I'll hide here in the cellar behind this door. Nobody will look in here for me. I'll stay here until darkness. Then you can bring a cloak, and we'll go out by the gate. Somehow we'll do it."

The boards came loose with a screech as the bolts pulled free from the mortar. The leather hinges were already rotted away, and the door fell outward. Catching it with his bleeding shoulders, Barabbas cursed under his breath. Vinegar Boy brushed the cobwebs out of the opening, cringing under the feel of them about his wrists,

"Aren't you afraid of scorpions or poisonous snakes?" he asked, and Barabbas chuckled. This time the laughter was not ugly or evil. "It has been said that Barabbas eats vipers for his breakfast."

He was still chuckling as he bent his back—with another groan—and crawled through the low doorway. Inside the cellar there was not room for a man to stand. He sat down with his back against the wall, his knees doubled up slightly.

"Board it up. The old hawk has never had a safer nest."

"Are you sure you will you be all right, Barabbas?"

"In the hollow of His hand He has me, boy. Jehovah, I mean. For the next few hours I intend to sit here counting His benefits. You are saving my life. May the blessing of God go with you."

The name of God didn't sound particularly foreign on the outlaw's lips. And though some of his violent language had caused the boy's face to burn, he had not really used Jehovah's name in vain.

Vinegar Boy set the bolts back into place on either side of the doorway, pressing small pieces of stone and broken plaster about them so that no one would notice that the door had been removed.

He knelt and peeked through the cracks. "Nobody will find you," he whispered. "I can hardly see you. I'll be back."

Then he picked up the gourd that had been lying in the stinking dirt. It felt cold and slimy, but the boy didn't mind. He would put it back on the fountain and run. Without doubt the death procession had reached the hill by now, and the men must have the vinegar. Most of all, Jesus must have it. It was wrong for such a good Man to suffer.

He put his hand on the bottle. The vinegar surged and chortled. The sponge at his belt, which he had almost forgotten, had picked up moisture from his garment. It flopped against his side like the head of a rain-drenched flower.

He stepped out into the sunlight, but there was no lifting joy.

7
THE ROAD NORTH

The boy darted through the crowd. If those who were lingering near the gates and the fountain saw the death detail as it passed, they gave no indication. Their laughter and their chatter filled the air like a gathering of magpies.

The sun was high over the city walls and getting warmer. On either side of the gates, inside and out, he noticed the patrols. Two by two the soldiers walked, their eyes running sharply over every person who entered or left, whether he was walking or riding.

Barabbas was right. The Roman legion was looking for him.

The boy wondered if any of the soldiers would notice the few faint bloodstains that had not come out of his garment. Most of the men from the fortress knew him well and were aware that he used the old alleys and unfamiliar ways about the roofs and walls. If one of them stopped him and inquired as to the wet, spotted garment, what would he say? He knew the strategy of the Romans well enough to realize that they would try to flush Barabbas out of hiding and send him straight through the gates to his death. It would be an easy thing for a soldier or two to claim they killed in self-defense.

Outside the gates, countless holiday booths of willow branches and awnings had been thrown together. All manner of enticements were offered to the pilgrims who might find their orthodox shops closed in the city. The air reverberated with the coaxing of the hucksters, and the bawling and blatting of the camels and donkeys in the caravansary, the courtyard of the caravan inn.

Ahead of him the road led straight north. Mile after mile of sterile highway stretched from Jerusalem in Judea to Caesarea on the coast of the Great Sea and east to the ancient city of Damascus.

Against the horizons the arched columns of the aqueducts marched across the valleys. Their grotesque shadows covered the land like giant, thousand-legged worms. Far to the northeast the snow-crowned Mount Hermon sat like a monarch with the bowed hills of Judea kneeling before him. Near at hand, a craggier hill thrust its shoulders upward. This was the hill called Golgotha. And on Golgotha the uprights of the crosses stood.

Wherever Rome went, the crosses went. They were as much a part of the dominion of Rome as were the labyrinth of roads and aqueducts, the hobnails and the whips, the civil orderliness and the pagan festivities.

With Rome had also come beauty of marble and granite and bronze, borrowed or stolen from Greece. About Jerusalem's bosomed hills, villas nestled in the midst of apricot and almond groves, vineyards, and rose gardens, where the lampreys and eels swam in the tiled pools and the goldfish darted like errant sunbeams in lily-lined ponds.

Hedges about the villas were often trimmed into fantastic shapes: satyrs with lyres, and statues of Pan with pipes; animals such as lions and unicorns, wolves and crocodiles.

Tropical birds swung like colored blossoms from their perches in the trees. Almost every villa owned its own beehive to provide golden sweetness of the honeycomb.

Vinegar Boy had been running. He was warm, and a stone had lodged in his boot. He found a bit of shade beside an arched iron portal, where he unlaced his boot and shook out the offending gravel.

On the lawn, several children played. They laughed and screamed with excitement as they threw a ball back and forth. One of the girls had long, dark hair, and her white dress floated about her ankles as she ran.

He wondered what she would say if he went across the lawn to her and asked for a drink. He had done that once. And the girl had screamed. She had taken one look at his face and cried out, and he had turned and run. He could still remember the hurt and the shame.

The memory brought the heat back to the birthmark, and he laid his cheek against the wrought iron of the portal. The fine ironwork had been done by an imaginative artisan. Diminutive cupids played hide-and-seek among the broad leaves. Fat clusters of grapes hung heavy with juice, which some of the mischievous cupids were squeezing into the cupped hands of their playmates. The whole of the iron gate had been painted. The cupids were golden and plump-cheeked, the grapes a glowing purple. They looked so real he could hear his stomach growl from thirst and hunger as he leaned against the green-veined marble columns in which the iron gates were set.

Then he retied his boots and entered the line of traffic. One stream headed for the city was composed of all types of conveyances, with people going to the Passover. But another line, thin and uneven, with everyone walking, was headed toward the place where the narrow dirt road left the highway and wound its thin, tortuous way up the crucifixion hill.

He could see the rocky promontory. The winds had cut caves in the face of the sandstone cliff, and the holes were like lifeless sockets. At the foot of the cliff, the stones had fallen away, leaving a wide depression that resembled the toothless grin of a dried skull. The skull-like characteristics of the cliff had given the hill its name of Golgotha, which meant "place of the skull."

News of a crucifixion always spread like some disease. Curiosity and thrill seeking brought many out to see the free show. In some ways the crucifixion was more exciting than the Roman theater or the circus because the men took longer to die, and spectators could participate to a small degree with their mockeries and petty torments.

At the place where the dirt road joined the highway, rough boards covered the gutter. Vinegar Boy stepped directly from the gutter to the boards and began climbing the hill. Ahead of him, a mother with a nursing baby talked with another woman who had left her house so quickly she had not taken time to fasten her long hair. She had brought no comb or pins, and the loop kept falling loose.

Their voices grated on him. The woman with the baby was saying, "At night, Hannah! At midnight, they arrested Him in the garden outside the eastern gate. Now, who would know where to find Him at that hour? I ask you. It had to be a friend."

"Of course it did."

"I told my husband time after time that they would manage to get Him sooner or later. They weren't about to let Him get away with what He was preaching."

Vinegar Boy felt a stab of remorse. When Jesus was arrested, he had been sleeping, dreaming that Jesus had put His hand on the birthmark and said, "Begone."

The pressure of the hand in the dream had been as warm and real as the sunbeams he had caught in his hands when he wakened. He could almost feel the pressure of the touch on his cheek. He thrust down the lump in his chest. If and when he could get to Jesus and ask the favor—if Jesus touched him, or even looked at him—perhaps he would cry. He always cried when anyone was kind. Nicolaus often teased him about it. "What a strange one you are," he would boom. "I do you good, and you weep all over me."

The women were still talking. "I suppose you heard what He did to the moneylenders the other day, Hannah? Whipped them right out of the Temple. Said they were making His Father's house a den of thieves. Practically caused a riot, I heard."

"The worse for Him. Nobody is going to threaten the Temple profits and get away with it."

"I imagine there is more to the whole thing than we will ever know."

"No doubt. The authorities only tell us what they want us to know."

"I don't believe half of what they say. Who does? It must not set well the way some of His friends insist that we have a Galilean king. And the rebels have been particularly active in the hills lately. My husband says that the fact that Barabbas has been captured hasn't slowed the revolutionaries down a bit."

"Do you suppose He was really one of them?"

The boy knew whom they meant, and he wanted to break into their talk and tell them what Barabbas had said, but he dared not.

The woman with the baby stopped. "Hannah!" she gasped. "You don't suppose He really was a rebel, do you? I mean, He could be preaching one thing and stirring up an insurrection at the same time."

"Our politicians do it all the time, don't they?"

"Oh, Hannah, you are a wise one!"

A man, whose profile seemed to be all nose, had fallen into step with the boy. He heard the women and snarled under his breath, "A wise one? She should be at home where she belongs. That Man had no more intention of becoming King of Israel than I have of joining Caesar's army. Dirty politics, it is. Something for our governor to boast about in his letters to Tiberius. 'I, Pontius Pilate, did arrest and crucify . . .'" The man pushed on, his sandals spitting up stones behind him.

"Humph! Who does he think he is?" the woman with the baby snapped. "He practically pushed me out of his way."

"And you with a baby in your arms too," the other woman consoled.

Vinegar Boy wanted to laugh. If he did, it would be ugly laughter like Barabbas's ugly chuckles. *Why don't you take that baby and go home?* he yelled silently to himself as he dodged past them. He could imagine what they would say if they caught sight of his dark cheek. They would have something else to talk about until the real excitement began.

Almost immediately he had to cut his stride because of two men and a boy walking ahead of him. The path was narrow, and the scraggy brush and thorned plants on either side made it impossible to get by. He pressed down his impatience and followed them.

Both men were richly dressed, and the sound of their garments accompanied their speech.

"They claim He was about to destroy the Temple," one of them was saying. "He boasted that if they tore it down He could rebuild it in three days."

The other man laughed. He used his hands in talking, and the sun flared on a green jewel. "Too bad Herod could not have had Him for a superintendent during the remodeling job."

"Can you image Israel with a Nazarene Messiah? Ridiculous!"

"The whole thing is ridiculous. How could any intelligent man take Him seriously? 'Before Abraham was, I am.'"

"Or, 'I and the Father are one,'" the other quoted in the same mocking voice.

The boy between them spoke. Vinegar Boy could not hear what he said, but the man with the green ring snapped back at him, "The Son of the Father? Why, the Nazarene is not sure of His earthly parentage, Enoch!"

The lad lowered his head, and Vinegar Boy saw his hands clench at his sides.

"You let your uncle and I do the thinking in this family, Son," the other man said.

Vinegar Boy found himself sympathizing with the rich boy's embarrassment. He was not allowed to think.

The older voice, arrogant and stiff, ran on. "When our king comes, Enoch, we will know it. The Romans will know it. He will tread upon Caesar's neck and make all our enemies His footstool. Remember your studies about Sennacherib, Enoch? One hundred and eighty-five thousand men destroyed by the Lord in one night. That slaughter will be as a dance in the marketplace compared to the coming of our Messiah."

Vinegar Boy had heard enough. Stepping aside into clumps of tough-bladed grass that cut his legs, he went carefully along the crumbling edge of the cliff until he had passed them.

Vengeance and death would not conquer the world. Nicolaus had said that goodness and gentleness would conquer, and Nicolaus was right. He had to be right. Violence bred more violence, as the flies of the field laid eggs that developed into worms that killed the leaves and destroyed the hops. And if the worms were not burned, they would become flies and start the whole cycle of destruction over again.

As he stepped cautiously along the edge of the cliff, he looked down. He could see the natural corral of thick shrubs and boulders where the Romans tethered their horses. The centurion's big stallion, Rubicon, was pawing the earth and shaking his head restlessly. The standard bearer was preparing to mount for his return to the city.

Vinegar Boy almost wished he had been a few minutes earlier. He might have asked to ride back with the officer who was next in rank to the centurion himself. The boy had never liked him much, but sometimes he was allowed to ride with him.

His boots had raised blisters on his heels, and he wished he had listened to Nicolaus when the steward warned him that the boots were too big. But the day was supposed to be full of *new* things—new face, new name, new boots.

The sole of his boot slid on a clump of bruised grass. One knee hit the ground. He scrambled up, knocking the dirt from his leg. The skin burned where it was chafed. He looked quickly at the bottle to be sure he had not harmed it. Above him, a strange silence held the hill. This was a stillness that he recognized. Below him, the anxious neigh of the big stallion cut the air, as if the horse could feel the wave of awful expectation sweeping the hill.

Vinegar Boy dug his toes into the path and dashed for the top. On the hill a wild, untamed roar of amusement broke forth. The boy knew that the prisoners had been led out into the center of the arena to be unclothed.

And as the hill reverberated with the cries of the spectators, the horse in the corral below let out a shrill, penetrating whinny that seemed to carry protest on the morning air.

8
THE
CRUCIFIXION

The plateau of the hill had turned into a place of confusion. Many of those who had come to enjoy the killing were like guests who moved about seeking a choice seat at a banquet. The boy compared them to vultures hovering and waiting, eager to descend with beak and claw.

He pushed through the throng to get to Marconius, and when he reached the arena he took in the scene with one glance.

The men were disrobed, but Marconius had allowed Jesus to retain his loincloth. The outlaws who had killed Romans and stolen from Caesar never received such consideration from the centurion.

The uprights of the crosses always remained in place in the center of the area covered with a smooth bed of river gravel. Iron supports, driven deep into the rock base of the hill, held the timbers solid. Weatherbeaten and stained, they scarred the shoulder of the sky.

At the northeastern edge of the hill, the cliff fell abruptly into the fertile valley below. A rude, doorless shelter housed the guards at this edge of the promontory. The old door had been made into a makeshift table on which the victims' clothes were piled. Later, after the clothing was divided by lot among the soldiers, the rations of wine, bread, and cheese would be set out for those who were ordered to remain on duty.

Two iron rings, fastened to the broken hinges of the doorframe, held the death lance. The vinegar bottle would hang on a peg beside it. When it was time for the sponge to be used, a branch would be cut from the old yew tree clinging to the southeast corner of the hill overlooking the stoning ground. The branch would be split at the end, the sponge inserted, and the ends tied together again. Then the sponge would be filled with the wine and raised to the blistered lips and swollen tongues.

The lance was used when the legs of the crucified men were broken to hasten their dying. This act was known among the Romans as the *crurifragium*. Then came the thrust of the lance beneath the ribs and into the heart; this was called the *perforatio*. The Romans considered the leg-breaking and lance thrust a merciful death compared to allowing the victim to hang on the cross for days to slowly expire from exposure and weakness.

As the boy's glance roamed about the hill seeking the centurion, he saw the woman with the baby pushing for a front seat on the boulders that had been cleared from the center of the hill and formed into a rude amphitheater on two sides of the arena. Her friend, breathing hard from the climb, had eyes only for the condemned men.

These women were among the common people

who always came to such executions. But as he looked about, he was amazed because today the crowd was different. There were Pharisees and Sadducees, stern-faced men with oiled locks from the Sanhedrin, which was the ruling court for the Jews in both religious and civil affairs. Priests were in linen robes, and the Pharisees had blue fringe about their skirts.

These men were among those who would shrink from eating off an unwashed platter, who would be defiled if they touched pork. But they stood together in this place of horror, rubbing their hands in evident approval each time a voice was raised in insults for the Nazarene.

One could not expect the outlaws' friends and relatives to crowd the hill, but where were Jesus' friends? Where were those He had healed? His mourners were few. Three women huddled under the skimpy branches of the old tree. Their mantles were about their heads, but the sound of their moaning could be heard.

Suddenly a cheer went up. The executioner had stepped from the shed. The sun shot fire from the mallet and the iron spikes in his hand. The crowd roared in anticipation. Among the men of the common people, the usual wages were being laid. Which of the condemned men would be the first to feel the nails?

Vinegar Boy saw Marconius step from the shed behind the executioner, and he pressed his way toward him. He lifted the vinegar bottle from his shoulder and started on a run around the inside edge of the arena. Another roar split the air.

Those who had laid their bets on the larger outlaw won. The four soldiers who had accompanied him in the march took their stations beside him. Their faces were grim; they were expecting trouble, and the crowd knew it. Tenseness gripped the hill. The boy let his eyes rise to the face of the doomed rebel. He was watching when the frustrated terror exploded into rebellious hatred. Each of the four soldiers made a swift grab for an arm or leg. The victim was lifted like one of Phineas's hogs and slung downward to the crossbeam so hard that the earth shook. The boy could hear the breath knocked out of him. Then as the air came back, the outlaw cursed and fought. He heaved and twisted, his muscles threatening to burst through the skin. The old sword scar broke open, and fresh blood dyed his ribs.

The soldiers laid the full weight of their armored legs against his forearms to hold his hands in place. Other soldiers ran to help and pressed his body against the beam. The executioner chose the spike. Silence fell.

Vinegar Boy rushed toward Marconius. "He hasn't had his vinegar!"

The executioner lifted his mallet. But Marconius spoke, and the hammer was lowered. A soldier reached for the vinegar. He snatched the wooden stopper out and thrust the bottle into the outlaw's mouth. He drank and choked. Vinegar ran out of his mouth and through his beard. The soldier tried to pull the bottle away, but the man's teeth had clamped about it. He took another mouthful. The executioner leaned over to place the nail, and the vinegar hit him full in the face.

The crowd roared in appreciation. The executioner would have smashed the man's skull, but one of the soldiers stopped him. The one who held the bottle tossed it at the boy and dropped on his knee to help restrain the struggling rebel.

The hands were prepared again. The mallet lifted.

Again the hill went quiet and tense. Vinegar Boy turned away, trying to close his ears as tightly as he had closed his eyes. This was always the worst moment of all—this first nail. The sickness and fear on the faces of those who would follow the first man were always terrible to see. But the sound could not be shut out. The hammer thudded and thudded again. Through flesh and wood the spikes sank deep. The cheers of the crowd buried the groans of the man.

Vinegar Boy opened his eyes to find himself looking upward into the frightened face of the golden-haired Dysmas. The young outlaw trembled. His body, straight and fluid as a statue, was marvelously brown. His hair covered his head like a rising sun. Sympathetic murmurs swept the crowd as he was led to his beam. Many grieved that such a body should be mutilated.

The young one did not struggle; he knelt first, his lips moving and his face toward the sun. Vinegar Boy knelt, too, offering the bottle. "Dysmas," he said, "here is your vinegar."

The outlaw showed no surprise that the boy should know his name. He drank deeply and gratefully. Then he laid himself back and held his wrists close to the wood. The spikes thudded. He moaned once as his body was yanked upward. He spoke to Arno, the Syrian officer, and Arno hailed Marconius.

"Captain! This one wishes to be hung so he can see the setting sun."

A murmur of support ran about the hill. Marconius was quick to assent. "He gave no trouble. Do as he asks."

So the younger outlaw hung on the outer cross facing west, and the middle cross waited for Jesus.

The Nazarene stood with His head lowered; drops

of blood and water stood on His forehead. His brown hair looked almost black where it was streaked with perspiration. His face was swollen and purple. Across His back and ribs the livid marks of the scourging crossed and recrossed.

Vinegar Boy wanted to run to Jesus, to beg the favor of restoration for his face, but he could not. How could he bother this suffering Man?

But deep inside the hope and the desire would not die quietly.

He would give Jesus the vinegar, and then maybe he would speak to Him as he had to Dysmas. Maybe if Jesus just looked at him, he would not need to ask, for Jesus would know.

The soldiers came forward, and the Nazarene went quietly. He spread His arms to the beam.

The boy fell beside Him and opened the bottle. Words struggled to come, but he could not utter them. The eyes of Jesus were closed.

Open them, open them, the boy pleaded silently. Words filled his head, but he could not speak. Oh, surely, surely, Jesus could feel his thoughts—such a little thing. Before the hands were nailed down, He could touch the stain and make it fair.

A soldier yanked the vinegar bottle from him. "We haven't got all day, boy," he growled. He thrust the spilling lip of the bottle against the lips of Jesus. But Jesus turned away.

The soldier grunted. "You'll beg for it before the day is over." He tossed the bottle back.

The executioner stooped, brushing his boots through the gravel to make a smoother bed for his knee. Jesus opened His hands and laid the wrists straight. The hammer sounded. Vinegar Boy could not turn his eyes away from the blood that filled the hollow of the Nazarene's hands. Two hands filled with blood as though they were Passover cups. Hands that had healed the lepers and restored the deaf. Hands that had plucked grain for His disciples and pulled the saw that helped to fill His mother's house with bread.

The beam was jerked upward. It fell into place.

Vinegar Boy threw his hand over his mouth and rushed for the hillside. Marconius was expecting it. His own face was white under the tan, and perspiration ran from his chin under the sweat strap.

"You should have left the vinegar and gone back at once," he said.

"I thought maybe I could ask Him, Marconius. But I couldn't. My throat was stoppered like the bottle. Why are they killing Him? Why?"

"They may be asking themselves that question centuries from now."

A wild cry arose above the other voices on the hill. It came from the path, and the centurion turned swiftly, alert. Arno stepped forward to block the rush of a young man who came screaming, "In the name of the Holy God of Israel, let Him down! Let Him down!"

The voice rose high and shrill as a trumpet. Vinegar Boy moved with the centurion. The other boy was larger and taller, but still a few years from being a man.

"Stand back!" Arno commanded.

"I won't let you kill Him! I won't!" He struck at the Syrian. Arno grabbed him about the shoulders and lifted him, kicking and screaming. He looked toward Marconius for orders.

The centurion hesitated, and Arno said, "We can't afford a riot, Captain."

Marconius nodded. "Shut him up!"

Arno dropped the boy, shoved him back with one hand, and slammed a fist into his chin with the other.

The boy fell, sprawled with his arms flung wide, his face to the sky. No one came to his defense. Vinegar Boy hunched down beside him. The fallen youth was fine-boned but sturdy, a faint fuzz of beard emphasizing the stubborn squareness of his jaw. His lips were full and red as a girl's, and blood trickled from the corner of his mouth. His fingers moved in the gravel as he struggled to sit up.

His thumb touched the tip of his tongue tenderly and came away with blood on it. "Cowards," he muttered, and Vinegar Boy did not know if he meant Arno and Marconius or someone else on the hill who should have come forward.

As the glazed look faded from the youth's eyes, Vinegar Boy saw that they were a gentle dusk gray. They were hard and angry now, but surely they could glow warm as hearth fire.

"Riot?" the boy said bitterly. "How could I start a riot? Where are those who would join me? Hiding like dumb sheep in my mother's feast room, that's where."

His face flushed. "What good am I? Twice they've mortified me like an infant. Last night I ran into the olive grove to warn Him, and they caught me and sent me home, naked."

"Who did?"

"The mob that was after Him. The Temple officers gathered up a bunch of riffraff to bring Him in. Are you His friend?"

"Yes—I wanted to be."

"I am John Mark of Jerusalem. Everyone calls me Mark except my mother. She's a widow. What's your name? I never saw you before."

"Everyone calls me Vinegar Boy. I live at the fortress with the steward. His name is Nicolaus. He raised me."

"My father's dead too. Haven't you got a mother?"

"No.

"Where did you get your name, Vinegar Boy?"

"I bring the vinegar to the hill. But mostly it's because I . . . I used to sleep in a vinegar cask—when I was little, of course. Here, let me help you up."

Their hands met. They were warm in one another's. Mark scrambled to his feet as Vinegar Boy considered him with an ache of envy. This was the kind of son he would like to be. Mark was handsome, brave, and good.

Brushing the dirt off his fine robes, Mark then raised his head. He had thick, brown hair that lay in heavy waves across his ears, and one hand after another brushed the waves back as his eyes narrowed.

"They must be doing something. Listen!"

There was nothing to hear. A strange quiet had fallen over the crowd. The hill had a feeling of oppressive stillness, such as foretells a storm.

A low muttering, like faraway thunder, ran through the edges of the rocky area.

The two boys pushed past the men and women who stood in front of them. A soldier was nailing a placard above the head of Jesus. This was the *titulus*, the title board that was always tacked over the head of the victim to inform the public of his criminal act.

The signs for the outlaws were simple and to the point: "Thief and Murderer."

But the sign being nailed above Jesus was unlike the others. Words were scrawled in large letters, large enough to be read from far off. Each line of writing was different, and yet the boy knew that the meaning must be the same. The signature of Pontius Pilate, procurator of Judea, was written beneath.

The storm of protest did not come at once. It took time for the meaning of the sign to break through. But when the understanding came, the hill shook with the varied furies.

Pharisees, who had been standing apart holding their fringed skirts against contamination, rushed forward. Their skirts were forgotten as their fists flailed the air.

Priests stooped and lifted what dust they could gather to pour over their oiled locks while they intoned lamentations and denials.

What the rulers and the priests started, the common people swept to a hideous height.

Under the uproar of the crowd, the boy thought he caught the mournful but ecstatic cries of the three women under the old yew tree. They were rocking themselves in a paroxysm of worship.

"Amen! Amen!" they cried over and over, tears running down their cheeks.

Nicolaus and Marconius had taught the boy to read the common languages of both Aramaic and Greek, but some of the letters on the sign appeared to be written with an agitated hand. Vinegar Boy was not certain of his reading. "What does it say?" he asked Mark. "Why is everyone so angry?"

Mark's gray eyes held a weird, hard light. "Pilate has written in three languages. He wants everyone to understand, and so they shall!"

Before he could be stopped, Mark had leaped beyond the line of boulders into the arena of fine stone. And beneath the cross of Jesus he began to yell. His arm lifted as he shouted the words in the language printed. He screamed into the faces of the Pharisees and the priests, the Sadducees and the soldiers. Into the faces of common laborers and tradesmen, he screamed, "THIS IS JESUS OF NAZARETH, THE KING OF THE JEWS."

The scribes and the Pharisees forgot their dignity and screamed back, "If He be the King of Israel, let Him come down from the cross, and we will believe Him."

"THIS IS JESUS OF NAZARETH, THE KING OF THE JEWS."

The priests screamed back, "He boasted that He would tear down our Temple and raise it in three days. Let Him now restore Himself, and we will believe Him."

"THIS IS JESUS OF NAZARETH, THE KING OF THE JEWS."

Even the common people joined in the tumult until the hill shook. "We have no king but Caesar. Hail, Caesar!"

Men advanced toward Mark, their faces black with fury.

"Mark, stop it! Come away!" Vinegar Boy begged frantically.

The soldiers moved forward, too, with angry faces, but they fell back as Marconius strode into the arena. His purpose was clear. He struck Mark twice against the cheeks. The marks of his fingers were white and then red as the blood receded and flowed back in high tide. Mark turned and stumbled through the crowd.

Vinegar Boy watched him go. They had been together only a few minutes, but they were friends. Now he would never see him again. Not once had Mark's eyes fastened in embarrassment or curiosity on his ugly cheek.

Vinegar Boy looked up at Jesus. He was lonely too. He hung friendless and forsaken against the bosom of the sky. The drops from the cups of Passover lay on the stones like dark petals drying in the sun.

9
MAGDALENE

Vinegar Boy sat with his knees hunched under his chin, his back against a boulder. Marconius stood with one foot propped on the rock while he fanned himself with the end of his cloak.

The first excitement of the crucifixion was over, and the hours of waiting lay ahead. Many of the spectators had gone.

The vinegar bottle and the sponge had been hung on the pegs by the door of the old shed. As the hours moved on—slowly and agonizingly for the men on the crosses—the victims would plead for water, and the sponge would be filled with the bitter wine. A reed for the administration of the wine had been prepared, as usual, from the slender branches of the yew. Sometimes the men used the piercing lance to lift the sponge, but Marconius preferred the reed.

During one of his earlier crucifixions a man crazed with pain and thirst had begged a drink. And when the sponge had been lifted on the spearhead, he had dropped his face suddenly with force. The spear had caught him full in the eye, piercing his brain. The soldiers had argued for weeks whether it was suicide or accident.

From where he was sitting, Vinegar Boy could see the rolled parchment under the sword belt on Marconius. He knew it was the order for the men to have their legs broken and the bodies removed before the Sabbath. Pontius Pilate was under orders not to aggravate the Jews in regard to their observances of the old Mosaic laws. The Jews would often go along peacefully enough under the bondage of a foreign power as far as their civil duties and liberties were concerned, but their hearts remained passionately loyal to the rituals and sacrifices that had come down to them from the time of their deliverance from Egyptian slavery.

Vinegar Boy looked toward the middle cross. The cross and the body seemed black against the bright sky. The title board creaked and swayed in the wind.

"He would have fixed my face, wouldn't He?"

"He still could, I think."

"But I couldn't ask Him to do something for me. Not when He is suffering like that."

Marconius dropped his foot and straightened. "I could if I wanted it as badly as you do. And if I knew my chances were going fast."

"I should have gone to the Temple yesterday. But the sprouts needed to be planted. We put in more than two hundred hills of hops yesterday." There was pride in his voice.

"That's good."

The title board creaked, and both looked up. The boy said, "Pilate shouldn't have mocked Him like that. Jesus never did anything to him."

"Maybe Pilate believes what he wrote." Marconius took off his helmet and wiped the perspiration from the cheek flaps with his fingers. "He didn't want to send the Nazarene to His death. I know, because I was there—from midnight on. Pilate is not clever enough to outflank Caiaphas."

"Why did the high priest hate Him?"

"Religion can make slaves of men, too, boy. And Jesus came to set them free, I think. He offered peace and freedom—and where is freedom for those who must constantly sacrifice?"

"But why didn't Pilate let Him go if he couldn't find anything wrong with Him?"

Marconius lifted an arm and pointed toward the city. South of them the towers and walls of Jerusalem glistened in the sun. And high over the place of the Temple the smoke hovered, signifying the sacrifices of the lambs in commemoration of the great feast. "It is not an easy thing to be a ruler of any people. And for this people it's exceptionally hard. Pilate is scarcely a big man any way you look at him. But he tried last night. I swear, he tried. The Nazarene refused to speak in His own defense. Pilate had to turn on Him in exasperation." The centurion's voice changed. Marconius could imitate other voices the way an actor in the theater did, and now his tones were petulant, arrogant, and worried.

"Why do You not answer me, Nazarene? Do You not know that I have the power to hold You or let You go? I can destroy You or set You free."

Marconius paused. "I do not think I will ever forget the look that Jesus gave him." Again his voice changed. Vinegar Boy could see the scene. Pilate, arrogant and commanding. Jesus, fettered and beaten. But the voice and the words when they came did not fit the picture.

"You say you have the power to release Me, but I tell you it is not so. For it was for this that I came into the world. You say that I am a king, and I say unto you that My kingdom is not of this world. But if it were of this world I could call ten thousand angels with swords in My defense. You have power over Me because My Father so wills it. And the fault lies not with you but with him who delivered Me unto you."

Vinegar Boy caught his breath. "Who did it? I mean, who *did* deliver Jesus to His enemies?"

"His name was Judas. That's as much as I know. A disciple, I think. But I don't believe that Jesus was speaking of Judas. I believe He was pointing the finger at the high priest who through his jealousy had planned for Jesus to die."

"Why did Jesus say He had come into the world to be arrested?"

Marconius looked down at him. "Again, I do not believe He spoke of fetters, but of the cross. He came to die."

Vinegar Boy searched the face of the Roman. Was he in earnest? How could it be? He knew about death. Everyone died. But it was something nobody wanted. Death was the end of all things—the rotten vegetables, the dead dogs, the funeral processions on the way to the tombs, the death carts rattling at night hauling the bodies of beggars and lepers to the valley of burning.

Was it possible that someone could be born into the world whose life's errand was to die?

The boy lifted a puzzled face. His left cheek was moist with perspiration, and the purple mark seemed to pulsate in the sun. Marconius was reading the Latin inscription on the sign. *"Hic est Jesus Rex Judaeorum."*

He said thoughtfully, 'That declaration may be the wisest and bravest thing Pontius Pilate will ever do."

"Then you think he really meant it?"

"Yes, I think he really meant it. "

As Marconius was speaking, an altercation broke out among the soldiers near the shed who were casting lots for the bundles of clothing. At the sound of rising anger in the dispute, Marconius clapped his helmet on his head and swung across the clearing. The gravel crunched and squealed under his boots. His red cloak brushed his ankles.

Vinegar Boy followed. Two of the men were arguing about the last cast of the die. The garment in question was the robe Jesus had worn. It was a notably fine-woven robe of white wool made in one piece without a seam. The robe was stained, but the fuller's art would restore both whiteness and softness.

One guard insisted that the robe could be divided, for such fine wool was valuable even in the piece. But the other claimed he should receive the whole garment.

Marconius picked up the robe. The material folded itself across his hand. A strange look crossed his face. The boy had a feeling that Marconius was arguing with himself. When he spoke, the men did not like it.

"Leave the Nazarene's clothing alone. If no one claims it, you will share according to your lots. I agree with Cloticus that the robe should not be divided."

The soldier named Cloticus grinned. He had a scar across his nose. The other men growled. Those who had won the sandals, the girdle, and the undergarment threw them back. The bloodstains on the clothing and the sandals made the boy remember Barabbas. Was he still safe? Was he thirsty? Had the insects or even the fever from loss of blood driven him from hiding?

"Roll up the clothing, boy," Marconius told him. "Surely some of His friends will ask for it."

Vinegar Boy doubted it. Where were His friends?

The women under the old tree were the only ones who grieved for Him. But even they had not come forward to comfort or caress Him.

He rolled the clothing into a tight bundle and tied a knot with the sleeves of the undergarment. He stuck the worn sandals under the knot.

As he worked, he sensed again a tingling expectancy on the hill. Marconius felt it, too, and was suddenly fully alert.

There was a movement on the middle cross. Jesus was trying to raise Himself upward for a deep breath. The agony of the effort caused drops of sweat to roll from His forehead. He moaned, and the boy looked toward the sponge and the vinegar bottle. Perhaps Jesus would take some of the drugged wine now.

But it was not drink He wanted. He was trying to speak. Even Marconius held his breath. The boy could tell from the way the Roman stood.

A hawk-faced man in dirty tunic and leather apron jumped on a boulder and cried aloud, "The Rabbi wishes to speak. Silence, all of you!" Then he made a sweeping bow. "Speak, O King. Tell us again how You can feed us on bread that will keep our stomachs filled forever. Tell us of the living wells that will flow from our bowels and we will never thirst again."

A titter ran through the crowd. Marconius swore under his breath, casting a furious glance at the spectators. He stalked toward the laborer, the sound of his boots on the stones offensive in the silence. Then he stopped. The whole hill was silent—an enforced quietness, for no one could speak though they desired to do so. From the silence, the voice of Jesus came.

"Father . . ." The word was like an oxen prick, and all eyes turned toward Him. "Forgive them." A nervous shudder passed over the crowd like wind over the heavy heads of ripened barley. "Forgive them, for they know not what they do."

Of all the things the people had expected Him to say, this was the most surprising, the most infuriating, the most condemning.

The words, like flint, struck fire in the tinder of their hearts, revealing each man for what he was. Some hearts melted in shame. Men and women turned and made their way down the hill. Others moved quickly, as if they had just recalled some urgent duty. Still others summoned what dignity they could as they left, but a high spot of color on their cheeks betrayed them. Some stayed.

A priest from the Temple moved forward. His hand rose over the people, as if in blessing. "Do not think that God hears this Man. He is a blasphemer. God does not hear sinners. This Man is not a son of Abraham. Rather, He is a servant of Satan and is this day getting His just recompense."

One of the women by the yew tree sprang to life. She rose to her feet, her voice ringing. "You lie! You lie! You who should lead us into light are leading us into darkness!" She ran forward. Her mantle slipped from her head, and a hand jerked it away. She grabbed it back and came on. Her hair, uncovered, shone in the sun—a wondrous copper-red coil that fell below her waist.

Behind her, another woman rose. "Come back, Magdalene! Come back!"

But the red-haired woman came on, her face blazing with anger. "You lie. You who boast that you know the Scriptures, have you not searched them for the Messiah? Have you not been told that He would come raising the dead and restoring the sick? Have you not seen my Lord's miracles?"

She turned to the crowd. "Do not listen to him. He will lead you to the slaughter."

As she fled past Marconius, his half-raised arm fell to his side. She went down on her knees at the cross, her hair brushing the stones where His blood was drying. "Slay them, Lord! Slay them!" Then she broke into sobs and buried her face in her hands. "No, Lord, no. I am ashamed. Should I not know how the demons work? Have mercy upon them, Lord. Have mercy." She grasped the wounded feet and laid her face against the cross. No one tried to touch her. The soldiers waited for the centurion to speak, but he stood silent, his eyes upon the woman.

The other women had risen and come to the cross. One was small and silent, the other short and heavyset with a rim of silver waves showing from beneath her headdress. She touched the red-haired woman lightly. "Come, Magdalene—come."

The one called Magdalene rose like a child and leaned on the shorter woman as she sobbed, "Oh, Salome. Salome."

The voice of the older woman murmured lovingly as they passed through the whispering crowd and back to the yew tree.

Vinegar Boy had raised his face to Jesus and he saw the Nazarene's eyes following the red-haired woman, and something crossed His face. Compassion, yes, but something more—an unspoken blessing. A promise of something wonderful in the future for the woman called Magdalene.

Vinegar Boy saw the look and read it rightly. Jesus had given Magdalene a gift she had not asked for. He felt a stab of jealousy. He should do as Marconius had urged him—ask for his favor. Surely Jesus would grant it. He must know how important it was for a boy to be the same as other boys—to have a name and a father instead of belonging to the garrison like the horses and the mules.

The bearded outlaw stirred, cursing. "Did she not say You could kill them all? Do it, fellow, and save Yourself and us. If you are the King of Israel, command that we be let down from the cross. Was it not for such a kingdom we have killed and stolen?"

There was a sneer in the words. Jesus did not look at him or answer him. But Dysmas, the bright-haired thief, spoke out sharply. "Have you no fear of God? We deserve our punishment, but this Man has done nothing amiss."

"Nothing?" screamed a fat member of the Sanhedrin from the farther line of seats. "Has He not made Himself equal with God? He has called us sons of the devil while boasting that He could make sons of Abraham out of the Gentile dogs."

Dysmas looked down at the well-fed ruler and lifted his nose as if he smelled something vile. "If you are so proud of being a son of Abraham," he called, "why have you not joined us in the hills? This Man is more a King than you are an Israelite."

A snicker ran through the crowds. The ruler turned purple. Then Dysmas struggled to raise himself, and with great effort he twisted so that he might see Jesus. He spoke clearly, but in painful jerks. "Lord . . ." The boy saw pain dampening the edge of his hair. "Remember me when Thou comest into Thy kingdom."

The nervous chuckle that had started through the crowd died. Vinegar Boy held his breath. *Dysmas had asked a favor of the dying Jesus.*

Would Jesus answer? He waited. The whole hill waited. Then Jesus replied, as though He were speaking from the broad porches of the Temple. "Verily, I say unto thee, today shalt thou be with Me in paradise."

The boy saw the eyes of the outlaw as they met and held those of Jesus. And in his heart the hope began to beat with a strength that shook his knees. Behind him, Marconius gave him a light shove.

"Go on," he said. "Ask Him. It may be your last chance."

10
JOHN
AND MARY

Vinegar Boy took a deep breath as he felt Marconius shoving him forward. Then he started across
the stony arena. At the foot of the cross he stood hesi-
tantly, filled with inner trembling. He reached forward
and touched the feet of Jesus. Lightly he touched
them—so lightly he could scarcely feel their coolness.
He touched the heads of the spikes, and the iron was
rough and sharp beneath his fingers.

Surely Jesus could feel the hope and the faith in
his fingertips. Nicolaus had said that the Nazarene
seemed to know all things; surely Jesus could hear the
plea his heart was begging.

Must he speak aloud?

He looked up. The eyes of Jesus opened. Their
glances met. Vinegar Boy could feel his heart begin to
pound. Jesus had *seen*. And now He would answer.

Please! Please!

A woman's cry snatched the eyes of Jesus away—a
forlorn, heartbroken cry that came from the dirt path

on the hill. Tears of disappointment burned in the boy's throat. But, like Jesus, he turned his face toward the woman and the man who were coming. As they drew near, Vinegar Boy knew he had never seen a browner face or bluer eyes than those of the man. The woman was muffled in garments. She was slender, and her ankles turned in the stones. The man was half carrying her. As they passed him, the boy heard the woman's sobs and caught the fragrance of a flower ointment. She collapsed at the cross.

Only the hardest of the hearts of the people on the hill remained untouched as they comprehended the depths of this woman's sorrow.

"Oh, my Son, my Son! How can I live without Thee? My house is left desolate. Oh, my Son, my Son."

Over the woman's head, Jesus moved and spoke. "Woman, behold thy son!" She raised her head, and Jesus nodded toward the brown-faced man. The meaning was clear, but to make it beyond doubt, He said, "Behold thy mother!"

"No!" she cried. "Oh, Emmanuel, my little One. Do not send me away. Do not make me leave Thee before Thou hast returned to Him who sent Thee. Oh, Emmanuel."

The man into whose custody Jesus had given His mother stared upward, grief and indecision on his face. Jesus nodded toward the city. The man pulled the woman to her feet. "Come," he said. "Come, Mother." Over and over he said it. Over and over she shook her head, twisting as he pulled her away. "John, I beseech thee. Do not make me leave Him. With what shall my world be lightened when the flame of His love is gone?"

John persisted, gently but firmly. She continued to cry that she would not leave her Son—her beloved Son—her promised Son—her Son of blessing.

Finally, John held her close against himself and spoke into her ear. Vinegar Boy would not have heard had he not drawn near, impelled by a desire to help. But he did hear, and it was among the little things he and Nicolaus and Marconius discussed in the weeks that followed the crucifixion. For the man with the leather-brown cheeks and the sea-blue eyes said, "Mother, He is no longer yours. No longer ours. He belongs to the world. Would you deny the world a Savior?"

The woman moaned and crumpled. John lifted her. He was strong but not tall, and her full skirts trailed in the dust. Vinegar Boy gathered them up and held them awkwardly. Marconius came and showed him how to wrap them tightly about her ankles.

John thanked them.

The centurion nodded toward the shed. "A bundle of His clothing is here. Would you like to have it?"

John nodded. Vinegar Boy ran to the old table and picked up the bundle. Cloticus, the soldier with the scarred nose who had been promised the cloak, gave him a surly look and followed a few paces behind. John looked at the bundle and shook his head. "I cannot manage it. I will have all I can do to get His mother back to the village."

Cloticus gave a pleased grunt and reached for the bundle. But Vinegar Boy stepped back. He thought of Nicolaus and the few old Gallic clothes in the chest. Nicolaus cherished his father's trousers and cap. Surely this woman called Mary would cherish her Son's clothing also. Words leaped from him unsummoned. "I will go with them, Marconius, and carry the bundle."

Something flashed across the Roman's face. A warning—an objection? "I don't think you should leave the hill."

"But they need me. She will want His clothes. I know she will."

"What about the thing you want?"

"I'll get back in time. You'll see."

"If there is any justice in the world, you will." But he shook his head as if he knew it would not be so.

At the top of the path, the boy looked back. Somehow he had hoped that Jesus might be looking at him as He had looked at Magdalene. But He hung with His head down, His dark hair covering His cheeks, apparently exhausted.

"Please don't die," the boy whispered. Then he slung the bundle of clothing over his shoulder and began to run. Below him, John was already carrying Mary across the wooden ramp that led to the paved highway.

When Mary came out of her faint, she was weak and had to be supported. John walked with his arm about her, trying to match his stride to hers. Vinegar Boy kept close beside her so he could help when she stumbled. John flashed him a grateful look each time, but neither of them spoke.

Once, Mary collapsed as she had done on the hill, and John laid her on the grass in the shade of a white-columned tomb, with her head on the clothing. The boy sat on the grass beside her and took off his boots. The blisters on his heels had risen and broken; he felt relief from their burning as he held them against the cool grass.

John began to talk. His voice was low and expressive, his words a bit ragged as if his speech was accustomed to being whipped by the winds. He talked with a charm that helped wipe the past hours' ugliness from the boy's mind.

He explained that Jesus was his cousin. Jesus'

mother, Mary, was his aunt, his mother's sister. "But so different they are. My mother is one of those who are on the hill."

Vinegar Boy thought of the three women under the old tree. "Which one is she?"

"The heavy, gray-haired one. The small one is called the 'other Mary,' and the red-haired one is Magdalene."

Vinegar Boy told John about Magdalene, how she had screamed that Jesus should slay them all, and then how sorry she was as she fell at His feet begging mercy for them.

John nodded. "Magdalene is a fiery one. Her temper matches her hair. Jesus freed her from the domination of seven devils, it is said. Yet, even so, she is as quick to storm as is the Sea of Galilee. Let an opposing wind blow, and—"

"Your mother quieted her. You are like your mother."

John raised his startling blue eyes. "If so, I praise God. She is a strong and compassionate woman."

John loved his mother. Perhaps this was why Jesus had chosen him to care for Mary.

"Sometimes my mother and I are accused of being softhearted."

Vinegar Boy smiled. "That is what everyone says about Nicolaus and me. Nicolaus is a steward at the commissary. He raised me."

"The people are right about you. Why did you choose to come with us?"

"Somebody had to. You couldn't do everything by yourself."

"But you did not want to leave the hill."

The boy was startled. "How did you know?"

John's eyes crinkled slightly, for even in the midst of sorrow it was John's nature to smile. "You have been anxious about the hill ever since we left. I can tell."

"All day I have been trying to get to Jesus to ask Him for a favor, sir. But each time I am near Him, I cannot speak." The ugly darkness was burning on his cheek.

"You wished to be rid of your affliction?"

The boy nodded. Would John think him selfish and unfeeling?

"If and when it is God's will, boy, He will do it. Have no fear. He knows your need. He knows the needs of all men. He sets our bread for us *before* we are hungry and wine before we thirst. "

"If He takes the mark away, sir, I will have to pick a name. I have promised Nicolaus." And the boy told John all the things that were on his heart. All the things he had told Barabbas in the dark dampness of the stairway, he told John in the midst of fragrant grass and sunlight. And when he was finished, John nodded with understanding. "We all carry affliction of one sort or another," he said. "What name have you chosen?"

"None. I do not know what I am, so I do not know what name my mother wanted. It must be the right name for me, sir—a good name because I will be the son of Nicolaus."

"Names are important," John agreed. "Jesus thought so. Would you believe that He called my brother James and me the sons of thunder?"

"But you are not at all like thunder."

"So it would seem. And I have pondered this. I am not a violent or noisy man. We have a friend who is both impulsive and wavering, and yet Jesus chose to call him 'the Rock.' It is plain to me, therefore, that names are meant not so much for what we now are, but for what we will be later on. He knows all things, and I have no doubt that the man of sand shall become rock, and my voice may be raised to warn of a wrath to come as thunder precedes the storm."

The boy listened. He did not understand all that John was saying, and he was eager for them to be on their way, yet he hated to have John stop talking.

Mary stirred, and John bent over her. She lay with her eyes closed, and her lids were blue with tiny veins. Her lips were pale, but faint color was beginning to show in her cheeks.

John brushed at a bee hovering over a purple clover in the grass beside her and sat down. "Yes, names are important," he began again as though there had been no interruption. "Even His name." He turned his eyes up toward the hill. "Did you know that the angel named Him Jesus? That means Savior. And the other —the name she called Him up there—Emmanuel. That means 'God with us.' Someday I will put yet another name to Him. It is here in the back of my mind, the word I wish to call Him . . . someday."

Mary struggled to sit up, and John sprang to his feet to help. He leaned over her. "Are you strong enough to stand, Mother? Perhaps you should rest a bit more."

Her voice was low. "Oh, John, what trouble I have been for thee."

"If you are trouble, Mother, may all my nets be full of it."

Vinegar Boy flashed him a look. So John was a fisherman—a fisherman from Galilee. He should have guessed it long before this, for who but the fishermen of Galilee had such brown faces and blue eyes?

The boy slipped on his boots. His feet had felt good in the grass, but now the blisters would hurt again. He picked up the bundle. Out on the highway, he turned again to look back at the hill, wondering if he would get back in time.

Please don't die!

John saw him looking and said, "Leave it in God's hands."

They did not go into Jerusalem as Vinegar Boy had expected. Before they reached the city, John led Mary down a side road toward a small village where the whitewashed cottages huddled at the foot of a hill like a flock of sheep. Tall palm trees, guarding the flock like shepherds, cast ragged pools of shadows on the narrow street.

They passed through a small gate, where a tinkling bell announced them, into an exquisite garden interlaced with paths of tiny creek-bed pebbles laid in cement. The pebbles shone like jewel dust beneath their feet. Bees hummed about the flowers, and birds sang from the branches of the flowering almond tree. Plots of herbs made patterns of varied green between the glistening paths.

A small grape arbor shaded a red stone bench near a spring where the water ran in a singing stream from the pipes into a miniature pool filled with yellow water lilies and purple hyacinths.

John led Mary to the bench beneath the tender green of the arbor. Vinegar Boy removed her sandals. John disappeared into the house with the bundle of clothing and returned with a mug of milk. He held it for her while she drank. Then he brought a towel, and the boy knelt by the pool and washed the dust from her feet. Her arches were latticed with a tracery of tan where the straps had not protected them from the sun.

How pretty she was. Her brown hair had a few

streaks of white. Her eyes, heavy with sorrow, were a soft shade of violet blue.

She drank the milk slowly as she stared straight ahead where a bed of long-stemmed poppies danced in green and red mosaic against a whitewashed wall. Tears flooded her eyes.

Vinegar Boy straightened up. "Please don't cry," he begged.

But John interrupted. "Tears will help her. Mother, weep as loudly as you will."

"John," she said softly, almost in reprimand. "Why do you call me Mother?"

"Because Jesus gave you to me to care for as long as I live. Do you not remember what He said?"

She shook her head. "It is as if a sword has severed me in half, separating my mind and my heart. I remember nothing but Emmanuel. All the things I have pondered and feared for my Son have come to pass. Simeon—you know about Simeon, John?"

He folded the mantle that had fallen from her head and laid it on her lap. "I remember what you have told us about him, Mother."

"The sword would pierce me too. Oh, Emmanuel, my little One. They will pierce Thee today, and I shall die." She put her face in her hands and bent her head to her knees. John comforted her with sounds like a drowsy sea. Vinegar Boy patted her shoulder awkwardly.

"Oh, John," she moaned. "Who will bring me the lilies of the field? Who will press the star flowers into my hands and tell me they match my eyes? Oh, Emmanuel, my Son!"

As Mary raised her head, her hand reached for the boy. Her fingers touched his hair, his cheek. Beneath her touch, he trembled, filled with a longing he had never known.

"He was much like you, little one."

"Oh, no, I am ugly. Ugly."

"He was not pretty, my Emmanuel. Not pretty, but lovely. Is it not so, John? Oh, yes, He was lovely. Always, always He was lovely. I loved all my children, for they were born of love, but Emmanuel *was* love. God's love. John knows. He can tell you."

"Someday, Mother."

"He knew He was going to die, didn't He? He knew. And He told us, but we did not want to believe. 'My hour has come,' He said this week in Bethany. But we would not believe, even though the funeral ointment filled the air."

Vinegar Boy listened and wondered. It must be true that Jesus had known that He was going to die. "For this reason I came into the world," He had told Pilate.

"Simeon warned me, John. Oh, so long ago he warned me."

John spoke over the head of the boy, explaining, "Simeon was an old priest in the holy Temple years ago. The Lord had promised him that he would live to see Israel's Redeemer. When Mary took Jesus there after His birth, Simeon lifted Him and declared, 'Behold the salvation of Israel.' He told Mary that her Son would be hated, for He would bring light to darkness, and men would see their evil and hate the light."

"When he handed my Baby back to me," Mary said, "he warned me of great sorrow."

John murmured, "Yes, Mother, we know."

He saw the boy waiting for him to go on, and he continued. "She has dreaded this prophecy: 'The sword that pierces Him will pierce thine own soul also.' Always she has lived with the fear of His death. During these weeks of tumult against Him, she has died a thousand deaths."

"He looked at my Baby," Mary said, "and he knew that He was the promised Child. The shepherds knew it, too, for they brought me word that angels had sent them to us in the stable at Bethlehem. There was no other place for Him that night—no place but a manger for the Son of God." Her voice faded.

John murmured words of consolation, and the boy laid his hand on her knee. "They came," she said softly. "Kings and wise men came, but I remember the shepherds best. So gentle they were with me, for I was young and knew nothing about giving birth. Like a lamb He was, in His swaddling clothes. Each of them touched His cheek, and one leaned over Him to sing, as if He were one of his own dear lambs, sick or frightened or cold. Such a kind thing he did! I have never forgotten him. For my Son, he sang." She began to hum, rocking as she sang. John turned away, his shoulders shaking with heavy sobs.

Vinegar Boy laid his head on Mary's lap. He felt the folded thickness of her mantle beneath his ugly cheek. So this was the way it would have been—the lullaby he had never heard.

The humming ceased. He felt Mary's hands beneath his chin. She lifted his face. Her eyes had lost their faraway look. She brushed his tears away with the mantle.

"How beautiful you are, child,"

Unbelievable, yet she had said it. "How beautiful you are, child." And in the silence, the bell of the garden gate rang.

11
THE TASTE
OF HATE

John greeted the tan, somberly dressed man who entered. Vinegar Boy noticed that the visitor's dark eyebrows were thick and bushy like those of Nicolaus, and the eyes that glowed beneath them were bright with wisdom. Mary did not look up as the men conversed in low tones. The boy caught a few fragments of the conversation.

"Pilate has given permission to take the body. It must be removed from the cross before the sun sets. Nicodemus and I will prepare it together. It shall be placed in my own tomb in the garden beyond the hill."

John came to Mary. "Mother, Joseph of Arimathea is here. He is a friend of ours. He is going to take care of the burial. Another councilor, named Nicodemus, is going to help. Mother, do you hear me? Is this to your desire?"

She nodded. Joseph moved nearer, and the men spoke openly. "There is the matter of preparing the body, John. I have linen and some spices that I wish to supply. Nicodemus has myrrh, but he would like to mix it with aloes. The shops are closed."

Vinegar Boy couldn't keep from speaking up. "Aloes, sir? Nicolaus has a store of aloes at the commissary. He uses them to revive the older hops. I'm sure he would let me have some."

"God be praised," Joseph said. "Nicodemus insists that this be his portion, but I will go with you to make pledge of payment in his name."

"Nicolaus will trust you, sir, and I can go faster alone. Should he bring the aloes here or take them to the hill?"

"To the hill," Joseph said. "The tomb is in the burial gardens beyond Golgotha."

But John disagreed. "I think you should come back here. If your steward cannot give us the supply, we may be able to get a pharmacist to open his shop."

Vinegar Boy knelt for a quick drink from the pool. He could see the reflection of his face in the clear water, the fair cheek and the dark cheek, and suddenly he was sorry that he had said he would go the fortress for the aloes. He should be on his way back to the hill. He had probably lost his chance for a miracle. The scourging had weakened the Nazarene, and He would not remain conscious as long as the big outlaw or the young one.

But there was no need to cry about the lost chance. Mary and John needed help, and Jesus had to be buried properly.

When he was outside the garden, he began to limp. His toes were blistering too. The highway back to the city was a channel of heat, and the stones, hot as griddles, burned through the soles of his boots. He ran when he could and finally entered the city by a small pedestrian gate east of the north portals. The gate opened on a crooked, sunless street, and he stopped immediately and unlaced his boots. Tying the latchets together, he draped them about his neck.

He could go directly to the fortress from here, or he could take the quicker, unlawful route that would take him past the alley where Barabbas was hiding. The stairs never frightened him as much when he was climbing them.

He wondered if Barabbas was still under the steps. He was probably suffering with thirst.

Vinegar Boy made a quick decision. He would take the quicker way and use the minutes he saved to see about Barabbas.

He began to run. Coming to a pink stucco tenement, several doors of which opened on the street, he dashed through the middle door and up the stairs as if he belonged there. Up three flights he went. The corridors were laid with cheap tile, and his feet slapped happily as he ran. Food smells came from the open doorways, and he heard a mother admonishing her child to "clean the radishes, not eat them."

His mouth watered at the thought of a crisp radish. The first hunger of the day had left, but the smell of the food brought the pangs back. On the third floor, at the end of the corridor, a window with a wide ledge opened to the flat roof of a lower story a few feet below. He crawled out on the ledge and was preparing to jump to the roof below when a woman came out of a door behind him and screamed like an angry camel.

"Thief! Thief!"

Vinegar Boy clutched his boots against him and dropped. Landing as lightly as Sparrow, he dashed for the outside stairway that led from the two-story dwelling into a courtyard below. A gate at the far end of the yard led into the street of basket makers and that street turned and twisted toward the dolphin square.

He had forgotten about the soldiers looking for Barabbas until he saw two of them patrolling the square. Slowing to a walk, he made sure that no one saw him as he slipped into the alley. After the fragrance of the small garden in Mary's village, the stench of the alley and the humid heat were almost overpowering. A stream of sunlight flowed down the broken stairway, and he noticed the line of ants making their way up the building.

Slipping behind the stones holding the steps, he saw that the old door had not been disturbed. The bars were still up, and his heart lifted in relief.

Pressing his face closest to the cracks, he whispered, "Barabbas?"

He heard a scraping sound, and a monstrous, hairy insect with an eye of red fire appeared in the crack almost against his face. He fell back with a gasp.

"Is that you, boy?"

Vinegar Boy drew a breath of relief. The "insect" was only the outlaw's eyebrow and bloodshot eye.

"It's me."

"So you *did* come back."

"I said I would. But I didn't come to get you. It isn't even noon yet. Are you all right?"

"Yes. What about your face, boy. Did he fix it?"

"Not yet. I haven't been able to ask Him. He did some things for some other people, though. I have to go back to the fort, and then I'm going back to the hill."

"How did it go with Dysmas?"

"He didn't fight. The big one gave them a hard time. But your friend asked if he could be hung so he could see the setting sun, and the centurion said he could."

"Listen, boy, can you do something else for me? I've always told Dysmas that I would see that he had a proper grave. There is a place in the hills where he always went at sundown. I can't take him there, but if you see that he has a decent grave, I—"

"I don't know anything about burying anybody. I never buried anything, not even a sparrow. But you don't have to worry about the birds getting him. They aren't going to let the bodies hang over the holiday. He'll be dead and off the cross by evening."

Barabbas cursed under his breath.

"I don't think you should worry about him, sir. He isn't worried. Jesus is taking him into paradise with Him."

Then he told Barabbas about the thing that had transpired between Jesus and Dysmas. After he finished, there was a long silence. When Barabbas spoke, his voice was fun of wonder.

"What kind of crucifixion is it where the dying can promise eternal life to another?"

"This whole execution is different, sir. Everybody on the hill knows it is different. I think it is Jesus that is making it so."

Another silence fell. Flies buzzed. The noise of the square was magnified in the confines of the alley. Vinegar Boy watched the line of ants making their endless trips up and down the side of the building.

Then they both heard the ring of hobnails. The boots stopped on the sidewalk near the opening into the square.

"Sh," Vinegar Boy warned Barabbas, and then made himself as small as possible in the shadows behind the stone columns of the steps.

From outside, one of the soldiers called to his companion, "Hold up, Theo. I want to check in here."

"Judging from the smell, you'll drown in a cesspool. Hurry up. I'm as dry as desert sand."

Vinegar Boy held his breath. Part of the sunlight was blotted out. He heard the scraping of the Roman's breastplate and the clank of the short sword as they rubbed the walls.

There was silence, and the boy knew that the soldier was letting his eyes grow accustomed to the dimness.

Then muffled steps came toward the stairs. A fly buzzed about the boy's lips, but he did not dare blow it away. He was afraid to move.

The soldier put his foot on the stone steps and started to ascend. When a rotten board bent under his weight, he stepped back quickly. From under the steps the boy glanced up. Sunlight from the upper level illuminated the soldier. The chin, seen from below, was hard and ruthless. Flakes from the rotten step sifted down. The boy closed his eyes. Something like the touch of fire stung his ankles, and he held back a startled cry. The line of ants was crossing his feet. He hated crawling things. He wanted to scream and slap at the ants, but if he did, he would betray Barabbas. He clamped his teeth. Then the soldier bent to peer behind the steps. Vinegar Boy seemed to shrivel within his rough, dark garment.

The soldier's partner yelled for him to hurry, and the armor scraped again as the soldier went back to the street. From outside, the heavy voice was pleasant. "I still say it is a good place to hide if you have the nose of a marble statue. Once more around, and we can have that mug of ale."

They were gone. The boy crawled out, stamping his feet and brushing at the ants.

"Have they gone?" Barabbas whispered.

"Yes."

"Can you take time to get me some water?"

"I don't know, sir. The gourds are all too big to get through the cracks of the door. And I can't take time to pull the bars off. If they see me bringing water—"

"Fill your boots. I'd drink water out of a dried rat's skin."

The boy hesitated. He did not doubt that the outlaw needed water. It would take only a few more minutes.

He slipped back into the street. The water in the fountain sparkled and sang as he drank. He had not known he was so thirsty. The water was warmer than it had been earlier in the day, and he rinsed his face and poured the cooling liquid on his raw heels. There were small red dots where the ants had bitten.

As he rinsed out his boots in the horse trough and then filled them with clean water, he felt eyes on his face. He looked up just in time to catch a woman's expression as she had a full look at his face. A flash of something hot and bitter and violent rose in his throat. Later he recognized it—the taste of hate.

A bread seller passed with a loaded basket balanced on his head. The fragrance of the warm loaves made the boy's stomach squirm in hunger. His look betrayed him. The woman hailed the tradesman. She said something to him about the "poor child" and thrust a coin into his hand. He handed her a loaf. She shook her head. "Couldn't bear to touch him," she said.

The man with the bread turned and yelled, "Hey— you there with the boots. Catch this. A gift from the lady."

The loaf spun through the air. Without thinking, the boy dropped the boots and grabbed for the bread. Then, as the boots fell and the water splashed, he snatched at them and missed the loaf. The tradesman laughed, and the woman began to complain about the boy's ingratitude and stupidity.

Suddenly he hated her. Worse than Phineas, worse than anyone he had ever known, he hated her. She was everyone who had ever laughed at him or looked at his face with pity, anyone who had ever hurt him and made him feel ashamed. She was all the men in the garrison who made sport of him and called him Liver Face, all the boys in the school who had caused Nicolaus to keep him at home and teach him the best he could.

Hatred choked him, burned his throat, was bitter on his tongue.

This was the way Barabbas hated the Romans—a killing hate. This must be the way the priests hated Jesus and wished Him dead.

The anger went as quickly as it had come. He shook with chills. The woman had gone, and the loaf lay in a puddle of water. He lifted it, tearing off the muddy part. Most of it was still crisp and warm. He laid it on the fountain lip and refilled the boots.

Anger had taken his hunger away, but Barabbas needed bread. He held the loaf under his arm and the boots in his hands as he went back into the alley. Bending under the steps, he whispered to Barabbas. The outlaw pressed his mouth to the widest crack, and Vinegar Boy poured the water slowly. Then he broke the bread and passed the chunks to him.

"It fell in the water. A woman bought it for me. She thought I was a beggar."

"No matter how you got it, Jehovah provided it."

"Barabbas?"

"Yes."

"I'm sorry I called you a murderer. That woman made me so mad I wanted to kill her. I know how it feels to hate somebody so much that you want to hurt them."

Barabbas stopped chewing. "I hope you don't know, boy. I hope you never know."

"I do. It makes you dirty and ugly all over. She saw my face, and she called me stupid. I wanted to kill her."

There was a deep silence. Then Barabbas spoke in a voice that might have soothed a sick child. "You cannot help the way you were born. There is nothing ugly or stupid about you." His voice was gruff again. "You've spent enough time with me. Get on about your errand. Do what you can for Dysmas, and tell him I would keep my promise if I could. And boy . . ." The softness was back. "If you ever need a father, other than your Nicolaus, let me know."

Vinegar Boy picked up his boots, swung the tied laces around his neck, and began to climb the steps. He went quickly, but with care, and when he reached the upper street he was smiling

12
BLOOD
OR INK?

Vinegar Boy's happiness faded somewhat as he approached the Fortress Antonia.

"Well, look who's back!"

The butcher stood in the doorway of the commissary with a bucket of fish in one hand and a scaling knife in the other.

"If it isn't little Liver Face himself!" He spread his legs to block the entrance.

"Get out of my way, Phineas," Vinegar Boy said. "I have to see Nicolaus at once."

The butcher sneered. "He's busy. I do believe this is the same ugly boy with the same ugly face who left here this morning boasting about a miracle. Have you picked a name to match your new face?"

Vinegar Boy pressed his lips together and scrunched down, trying to squeeze past the butcher's legs. Phineas swung the bucket from side to side, nose-high to the boy. The nauseating smell of slightly ripe fish hung in the doorway.

The boy pulled back and said, "Phineas, I'm warning you. Get out of my way."

"Make me, you little—" The ugly name was spat like venom from between yellow fangs, and Vinegar Boy lowered his head and charged. He caught the butcher in the pit of the stomach and sent him stumbling backward. The bucket flew out the door and hit the bricks, scattering fish in the thin dust.

Phineas let out a howl of rage and surprise as he was bowled over. Flinging up his arm, the scaling knife flashed across the boy's chest. The boots saved him. The blade glanced from the hard toe of the boot to his arm. He felt the fiery slash and screamed.

Nicolaus seemed to appear out of thin air. He caught the whole story in one quick glance—the boy's frightened face, the blood oozing from his arm, the butcher on one knee with a furious look on his face and the knife clutched in his hand.

Nicolaus bellowed. He lifted Phineas with both hands and slammed him into the wall. Phineas's eyes popped, his face mottled with red and purple. Vinegar Boy screamed, "No, Nicolaus! No! He didn't mean it. I'm not hurt."

Phineas had let go of the knife and was clawing at the steward's hands. Then Nicolaus dropped him like a bag of pig husks, and the butcher collapsed on the doorsill, his face as clammy as one of his own plucked fowls.

The steward examined the boy's wound with care. The cut was not deep. He squeezed the flesh gently to let the blood run freely.

"It really wasn't his fault, Nicolaus. I had to see you in a hurry, and he wouldn't let me through the door. I butted him down. It's only a scratch."

Nicolaus insisted on cleansing the wound with turpentine and putting ointment and a bandage on it. As he did, the boy told him why he had come back to the commissary. As he explained that Jesus was the third man to be crucified, the steward's blue eyes filled with tears. "The fools. The fools. They kill the vine of goodness and let the wild grapes flourish." And then, "I'm sorry, boy."

"There is still time for Him to help, Nicolaus. I just haven't been able to ask Him yet. Marconius says He will have His power until He dies. And he is right. If you were up there you would see."

The steward listened as the boy told him quickly about John and Mary and Joseph of Arimathea and the need for aloes.

"I told them you would let us have some. Nicodemus is going to pay for them."

The steward shook his head. "I can't give them warehouse aloes, boy. Besides, our supply is all in hundredweight jars."

Vinegar Boy was certain that he had failed to make himself clear. The aloes were for Jesus, the Man of goodness, whom Nicolaus admired. And the steward did not have to *give* the aloes; an honorable man intended to pay for them.

"But I am also an honorable man," Nicolaus said. "I cannot sell garrison stock without proper authority."

"Just this once?"

"If Nicodemus were to appear before me this instant and offer me twice the market value for the jar, I could not let the aloes go. Not without an order from the tribune or the governor."

"There's no way you can manage it—just once?"

Nicolaus shook his head. "I'm sorry, boy. If they were mine, you could have them. This has been a disappointing morning for you, and I'm sorry. " He tied the knot in the bandage and held the brown hand in his own. Seeing the entreaty in the amber eyes, his own pale blue eyes misted, but he shook his head.

"You'd be doing it for Jesus, sir."

The bald head with its fringe of stiff, white hair shook again.

"Then will you go with me to the tribune and help me explain? Maybe he would—"

"Son, you know Rome better than that!"

"But I promised!"

"You were not thinking before you spoke."

"But Jesus would have healed me. He might do it yet if I get back before He dies. Please, Nicolaus. He *needs* the aloes."

"No. The answer is no, boy, and that's final." Phineas had gathered up the scattered fish, and, as usual, he had managed to hear the conversation. He passed them with a smirk and said, "Let the fellow rot. It's no more than the rest of us have to look forward to."

Vinegar Boy raised blazing eyes. "He is not going to rot! He is going to paradise! He said so."

Nicolaus put his hand on the boy's shoulder. "Quiet, son. He is right; man returns to the dust."

"Maybe you should come to the hill, and then you'd see! You've never seen a crucifixion like this one. This isn't just an execution. Jesus told one of the other men on the cross that he would be with Him in paradise today. Nobody rots in paradise. Rot is for dogs . . . or fish." He glared at Phineas, who stood in the hallway holding a fish by the tail and grinning. "You'll rot, too, you nasty old thing."

Nicolaus thundered, "That's enough, son!"

But the frustration of the morning would not be held back. Vinegar Boy turned on Nicolaus. "Don't call me your son. I'm not your son. I don't belong to anybody. I am just what he has always called me—a liver-faced bastard!"

The words burned like coal on his tongue, and when they were said, his lips were blistered and defiled.

The steward's blow rang in the quiet corridor. The blood left the fair cheek and then came back as red and furious as the colors in the dark cheek. The boy could not believe that Nicolaus had struck him. Never in his life had Nicolaus struck him.

He raised his eyes—hurt, startled, confused. Nicolaus stood ready to gather him to his chest, but the tears that sprang into the amber eyes were angry tears.

"I'll get you an order for your old aloes. I know who will give it to me. He believes in Jesus even if you don't."

The idea had come almost as quickly and violently as the slap. The words tumbled over one another like grasshoppers. "I'm going to Pilate. He didn't want to kill Jesus; he thinks He is the King of the Jews. He said so. Just you wait. I'll be back."

Before Nicolaus could restrain him, Vinegar Boy was gone. The steward's shout echoed in the garrison grounds. In the doorway the butcher cackled with laughter.

In the boy's breast shame burned as deeply as determination. Nicolaus had struck him, and Phineas had seen it. This was the depth of humiliation.

He cried as he ran. He had been sent many times to the palace quarters in the fortress and had spoken to the governor as Pilate reviewed the troops or walked with his wife, Procula, on the balconies and porches. He liked Procula. He would find them. One did not burst into the governor's chamber without cause, but he had cause, and no one was going to stop him.

He dashed up the marble steps and through the

bronze portals, past the door porters who yelled for him to stop. Down carpeted corridors he fled, between heavy brocaded curtains, across wide mosaic chambers. He darted under the arms of guards and chamberlains who made attempts to grab him.

Some who spoke of him later swore that he was a white-faced imp with eyes of blazing gold. Others, who glimpsed the dark side of his face, argued that he had been a demon of darkness under whose skin blue and purple flames burned. His eyes had not been golden fire but dark red coals.

Still others who saw the racing boy and the look of urgency upon his wet face felt their hearts constrict. Surely this child had come with some great petition to the governor. Perhaps his father had been ordered to the gallows, or his mother was dying for want of medicine or bread. Or perhaps a sister, beautiful and pure, had been snatched from the safety of the family. Whatever it was, they wished him well as his pounding feet carried him out of sight.

For themselves, they went back to their daily tasks, knowing this was a bad day to sue for favors. Pilate had confined himself to his private bedchamber with a severe headache. He had called several times for basins of water, hot and cold, to bathe his brow. Only a few knew the truth. The governor of Judea, after turning Jesus of Nazareth over to the high priest, Caiaphas, to be crucified, had felt the pangs of conscience so severely that he was having mental upsets. He believed that his hands were covered with blood, so he dipped them constantly into the scouring ashes, the water, and the oil.

Procula, his wife, bent above him, speaking comfort, but her own black eyes were dead as week-old cinders. She was as stricken as Pilate.

"I warned you. Oh, Pilate, my husband, I warned you. If only this once you had been strong enough to face up to them. This was a religious quarrel, and you had no right to interfere. My dream came, and my message was sent to save you from this infamy. 'Have nothing to do with this just Man, for I have suffered much in a dream concerning Him,' I warned you."

Pilate quivered and washed his hands again.

Thus it was that the boy found them. He wasted no time in greeting, though he had heard the long and honorary salutations many times. He stopped in front of them, breathing fast, the tears on his cheek, the cut on his arm throbbed with every breath, and the bump on his head throbbed in unison with his arm.

"Please, sir," he said as he went directly to the chair where Pilate slumped. "You must help me. You have given Joseph of Arimathea permission to bury Jesus of Nazareth. But we need aloes for the embalming. There are aloes at the brewery, sir."

Procula' s hands moved nervously across the front of her garment. The robe was of soft, green silk spotted in the front with water. Her nose, too large for beauty, was pinched and white in the middle of her tense face. She spoke to Pilate. "You have given Him to His friends for burial? You did not tell me this."

Pilate said nervously, "There was nothing definite. I told him we would see. I have no objection—"

Vinegar Boy rushed on. "Sir, Joseph is going to take Him as soon as He is dead."

Pilate looked up. "They must bring me proof. The centurion must send me proof that He is dead. This I insist upon."

"He will be dead, sir. He is dying now. They will bury Him in the garden beyond the hill where the cypress trees are. I live with Nicolaus at the commissary and I—"

Procula said, "We remember you."

"Nicolaus won't let me have any aloes without an order, sir. They are in jars of a hundredweight."

"Am I never to be rid of this fellow?" Pilate murmured, almost to himself.

"Look, boy." He held out his hands. "See? I can't get the blood off. I have tried and tried, but it will not wash off."

The hands of the governor shook, but the boy could see no stains or blots, not even under the trimmed and polished nails. Looking into the quivering face and the colorless eyes, he understood. He looked at Procula, and her lips trembled.

Vinegar Boy had seen this kind of illness before. Once a young recruit had returned from a foray against the rebels in the hills and had sat for days in the sun with his hands trembling and a strange blueness about his lips. He would rub sand into his hands until they were raw, trying to remove the guilt of shedding human blood.

The boy looked at Pilate's hands and said, "Yes, sir. I see it."

Pilate did not argue with the young recruit, but the boy tried to give him something else to think about.

"Are you sure it is not ink, sir?"

"Ink?" Pilate stared. "Ink?"

Procula fastened her dark eyes on the boy, and he flushed. "Don't you remember the sign you wrote, sir? The one that said, 'This is Jesus of Nazareth, the King of the Jews'? You sent it to the hill, sir. You signed it in ink."

Pilate lifted his face. "I did. So I did. I had forgotten. They wanted me to change it. Caiaphas, the fox, practically ordered me to change it to read that Jesus had *said* He was King of the Jews. But I told him that what I had written I had written. You see, wife, I can stand up to them when I so desire."

Procula's tears washed over her face. Pilate said, "Have them fetch me another basin. Ink should not be difficult to remove."

He thrust a finger toward a desk in the corner of the room. "Fetch me my writing materials. You shall have your order for the aloes. Tell them it comes as a gift from Pontius Pilate."

Vinegar Boy fetched the materials. His heart pounded. "Thank you, sir. You have done enough for Him. They are saying on the hill that the sign is the wisest and bravest thing you could have done."

Pilate's lips lifted. He held the pen in a steady grasp. "Did you hear, Procula? I have done well. Now . . ." The pen scratched. "Aloes from the warehouse—a hundredweight jar. There you are. Procula, hand me the basin."

Vinegar Boy ran out as he had run in. This time he clutched the precious order against his chest. He had not failed John and Mary. He had not failed Jesus. And maybe if he hurried, Jesus would not fail him.

13
MASTERS IN ISRAEL

Nicolaus chose a small, hand-drawn cart from among those used for commissary produce for the boy to use in hauling the jar of aloes to the hill.

The steward had accepted Pilate's order, entered it in the books, and put the charge against his own name in the account ledger. Vinegar Boy protested. "You aren't supposed to pay for them. Joseph said his friend would."

"We will see about it when the time comes," Nicolaus said reasonably. "It may be that before this day ends we will wish to make the aloes our own gift to the Nazarene."

"But even if He fixes my cheek, you don't have to pay. They are worth a lot of money."

"So is the boy who is going to be my son," the steward said, and his pale blue eyes warmed with tender thoughtfulness. He lifted the jar in his heavy arms and walked with a bowlegged stride to the cart. He placed the jar carefully in the bed of the vehicle which, though small, was strong enough to haul a man.

"Can you manage alone?" he asked. "We have barely started on the inventory, but I can send someone else with—"

"No, Nicolaus. Please. I want to do it myself."

"It is a good thing you are going. Do not be afraid to ask a favor for yourself."

"I won't. I've made up my mind."

"Has it not been said that the Nazarene chided His friends, telling them that they had not because they asked not?"

The boy nodded. A bright smile made his amber eyes clear as honey.

"Watch the ruts, boy. These carts tip easily."

Vinegar Boy was careful, choosing the streets with the smoothest pavements. There was no way he could shorten the route from the fortress to the north gate this time. But no matter how careful he was, or how slowly he went, there were places where the cart tipped and slid, and the heavy jar smacked against the sides and end of the cart. Each time, his heart would come up into his throat, and he examined the aloes with care.

He had no idea how much money would be wasted if the cargo of pungent leaves and aromatic twigs should be scattered in the dust. Nicolaus had explained to him that these leaves and twigs were from a valuable plant that grew far away from Jerusalem. The pharmacist at the fortress would extract the juice from the leaves and the twigs and use the dried juice as a purgative and tonic for the troops. But the dried leaves in the larger jars were used with the hops to help with the making of the beer. The aloes in the jar would be crushed fine and mixed with the myrrh that Nicodemus had. Then the winding clothes would be impregnated with them, and the body of Jesus would be preserved for a while.

Vinegar Boy did not know how much Nicolaus had charged against himself for the aloes, but it must be a considerable sum. Aloes were for the wealthy. Nicodemus was making a kingly gift to the Nazarene.

The cart wheels began to whine and groan, and the boy told himself to remember to tell the wagoner at the fortress to grease the cart axle.

The blisters on his heels were hurting again. He had not taken time to exchange the boots for his sandals; there had been too many other things to think about. His fight with Phineas, and his quarrel with Nicolaus, and the visit with Pilate.

The cart jolted, and pain shot up his legs. His head ached from hunger. Marconius had told him that the first pangs of starvation were always the worst. After several days of not eating, a man could live on a few sips of water and a couple of grains of corn.

He was thinking about Marconius, and wondering what was happening on the hill, when a mule-drawn wagon thundered up behind him. The driver had come from outside the city walls, and as his wagon hit the main highway, he rose and cracked his whip as though he was in a hurry to be gone. A Roman horseman patrolling the traffic turned and bellowed an order at two foot soldiers. The soldiers raced forward, yelling for the driver to halt.

When the soldiers yelled, the boy stopped too. The cart rolled up against his heels, and he bit his lip with pain. Then he saw the wagon, and fear filled him because there was a dirty cover over the wagon bed, and under the cover he had seen a heavy movement.

Had Barabbas been foolish enough to attempt to make his own way out of the city in broad daylight?

The soldiers approached the wagon with care. One used his sword to slash the rope that tied the corner of the tarpaulin. Then, flipping the cover back, he held himself ready to lunge. The other soldier stood equally alert.

The cover flew back and an angry grunt came, followed by a series of excited squeals.

The lump in the boy's chest dissolved, and he giggled in relief. The wagon held only a nursing sow and several piglets.

The soldiers sheathed their swords and motioned the driver on. One said, "Not the Jewish pig we were expecting, eh, Servius? Cheer up. He'll be out sooner or later. He can't stay holed up forever."

Vinegar Boy drew a deep breath and remembered that he had not thought to tell Nicolaus about Barabbas. As soon as he came back he would tell him. Nicolaus was honest and fair; he would probably help him get Barabbas out of the city, for he would know that Jesus had really died in Barabbas's place.

But Nicolaus would have to consider all sides of the question before acting. He always did. He would insist on the boy considering all things too. Nicolaus never served up an opinion as if he were ladling out a plate of greens, saying, "This has satisfied me. Eat and be full."

But the talk about Barabbas and his escape from the Romans would have to wait for evening.

Now he had to get the cart to John and get back to the hill. When he reached the road leading to the small village of palm trees, his hands were blistered. The wound on his arm throbbed, and for the second time he felt the bruise on his head where he had fallen against the stones in the alley after his first meeting with Barabbas.

When he reached the gate with the tinkling bell, he was hot and tired and thankful for the cooling shade. Joseph was pacing up and down the garden walk, his dark robes whistling. John, who knew the fisherman's patience, sat on the bench under the arbor. He rose quickly when he heard the cart outside the gate.

Vinegar Boy looked for Mary, but she was not in sight.

A third man stood in quietness near the pool. He was shorter and heavier in the middle than John or Joseph. His face was small, his neck thin. He reminded the boy of a scholarly turtle. On his bald head he wore a richly embroidered black skullcap, and his ankle-length robe of lustrous black-and-yellow-streaked silk covered a white garment.

"Praise God you have the aloes," Joseph said. His robes were fine, black wool, with a line of blue silk bordering the hem and sleeves. A turban of the same shining silk was ornamented with a pin that flashed blue fire in the sunlight.

"Where in all of Jerusalem could we have obtained such a supply on a holiday?" Nicodemus breathed. "Jehovah-jireh."

"Aye, Jehovah does provide," Joseph said.

"Praise the name of Him who never forsakes us." Nicodemus sounded like a rabbi. Vinegar Boy had slipped into the Jewish synagogues several times to listen to the Hebrew teachers, because he was always curious about the Hebrews' God. There was a completeness about the Lord God Jehovah that was lacking in the gods of the Romans and the Greeks. The Jews believed that their God, though invisible, was always present in all places at all times. He ruled men with patience and justice.

Nicolaus did not disagree with them. He believed

in a Creator whose hand had formed the world from nothingness, and in a just God who would recompense evil for evil. He had seen that men who plowed iniquity and sowed wickedness also reaped the same.

Vinegar Boy noticed that John the fisherman listened to both Joseph and Nicodemus with great respect. While Joseph seemed wise and used to speaking with authority, Nicodemus seemed more wise. Both of them were probably so learned that they were among those whom the common people spoke of as masters.

John pulled his robe knee-high and thrust the material beneath his leather girdle. The boy noticed his powerful legs as he stepped in front of the cart and reached both hands to the handle. He bent forward, and the cart moved.

Vinegar Boy said, "I can pull it, sir."

John shook his head. "You have done enough."

"But you'll get blisters, sir."

John held out a palm and smiled, and the boy flushed in confusion as he ran alongside. Calluses thick and old covered John's hands; his fingers curved with strength.

Joseph said, "You will find no stronger hands in Galilee, boy, unless they be the hands of Peter."

"Peter." Nicodemus repeated the name sadly, shaking his head as if in sorrow.

John said, "Do not forget that one of the last things Jesus said to us was that the world would know that we are His disciples if we love one another."

The wheels of the cart moaned, and the shade of the palm trees was left behind. All four lengthened their strides.

Vinegar Boy wondered, *Who is Peter? Evidently he is someone who should be here with John but isn't.*

As John pulled, Vinegar Boy tried to imagine how

he would look on the deck of his fishing boat. His long ,brown hair would be wet from spray; his bare toes would grip the wooden planks. The muscles of his arms and legs would swell as the net broke water, and the fish, like glittering half-moons, would jump as they tried to get back into the sea. The spray, falling back in the blue sunlight, would be like blue wool woven with threads of silver mist.

Once, he and Nicolaus had made a trip into the Galilean country. Nicolaus had gone to make arrangements for a supply of fresh and salted seafood for the commissary.

Both of them had been excited as they stood on the fishing docks at Capernaum, on the western corner of the blue sea, and watched the catch dumped, gleaming and glistening, into the baskets of the fish sellers. Later, in the marketplace, the boy had been dismayed to see that the beautiful colors had faded. The eyes that had shone like jewels in the sea were cold green like those of the butcher.

The small cart bounced, and the boy sprang to brace the jar. He considered the two men who walked, one on either side of the cart. Nicodemus went with his hands behind him, his thin neck thrust forward, the breeze billowing his cloak. Joseph moved more freely, with his arms swinging wide as if he had once cast seed.

Nicodemus turned to face Vinegar Boy. "What do I owe your fortress friend for the aloes?" he asked.

"I don't know, sir. He put them against his own account, although I told him you would pay."

"So I shall. After the Sabbath."

"He might not take your money, sir. He said something about paying for them himself."

"Does Jesus of Nazareth mean something to him?"

"Nicolaus is not a Jew, sir. But he did believe Jesus could do miracles. And he admired Him for His goodness."

"I will call upon your Nicolaus and thank him. Then I will tell him much that he needs to know about the Nazarene. Your steward is a long, long way from the full truth."

It seemed that Nicodemus was criticizing Nicolaus, and the boy's exasperation showed. "If Nicolaus wants to give you the aloes, sir, you'll have to take them. Can't you understand when somebody is going to *give* you something?"

Nicodemus gave him a strange look. He felt his cheek burning. The cart slowed, and John turned, for he had caught the angry tone in the boy's voice.

"I'm sorry, sir, I had no right—"

But Nicodemus was not angry. A slight smile lightened his dark face as he looked across the cart to Joseph. "The boy could be right. Perhaps none of us recognized the gift when we saw it. We were supposed to be leaders in Israel, but fishermen and farmers were more ready to accept."

Joseph nodded. "God loved us enough to send Him, and we refused Him. Had I but bowed to Him in public, or extended my hand at the Temple, I could more easily bear this hour."

John spoke. The whine of the cart was loud and monotonous, but the fisherman had learned to pick up the sound of voices over the roar of the sea or the snapping and cracking of the ship's rigging.

"You did a brave thing when you asked Pilate for the body."

"Even so, John, I must confess that I based my plea upon the right of a rabbi to receive a proper burial. I should have claimed Him for what I now believe He is—the Messiah."

Nicodemus said, "Pilate would have denied you then, and what would you have profited?"

"Even now the governor could change his mind," John added.

Vinegar Boy said, "1 don't think he will. I think he believes that Jesus is your king. But you will have to prove that He is dead before you take Him away! Marconius will do that for you."

John halted the cart while he wiped perspiration from his eyes. "And who is Marconius?"

"The centurion at the hill—the one who gave you the clothes. He didn't want to hurt your friend; he understood why you followed Him."

The heat of the day was becoming oppressive. There seemed to be no breath of air. The heavy folds of Nicodemus's robe fell straight about him. Vinegar Boy took time to pull the heels of his boots away from his blistered heels. As they rested, Nicodemus spoke. His words hung in clusters, full and bursting with the juice of bitterness.

"Shall I ever forget His reprimand? 'Nicodemus, thou art a master in Israel. Dost thou not know why I have come and from whence? Knowest thou not that eternal life lies not in flesh and blood but in the spirit?'" Tears glistened on the brown face. "I, in my wisdom, knew so much and understood so little."

Vinegar Boy lowered his head. He knew the embarrassment of deep feelings, and the small man was feeling deeply.

"He looked at me that night on the rooftop. His countenance shone bright as the lamp of heaven. 'Nicodemus. Nicodemus.' Oh, I tell thee, John, He was not far from tears that night. 'Know ye not that a man must be born again before he can see the kingdom of heaven?' Even this child knows that one cannot pass the second time from his mother's womb, yet I asked Him that in my stupidity."

Joseph remained silent as John picked up the cart handle.

"But that was not the fullness of my blunder, friends. I understood even less when He spoke of being lifted up. 'As Moses lifted up the serpent in the wilderness, even so must the Son of man be lifted up: that whosoever believes in Him should not perish, but have eternal life.'"

No one spoke. Their eyes went to the hill ahead of them where the black marks of the crosses marred the sky.

Vinegar Boy thought about what Nicodemus had said. He could imagine it the way it was the night when Nicodemus had gone to find Jesus on the rooftop. Jesus would have been resting because His days were always full of healings, and His hair would be lifted by the wakening breeze. A full moon would be flooding the world with light. Nicodemus would climb the stairs slowly, his hands behind him, his robes rustling in the darkness like the wings of a settling bird. Jesus would know that he was coming and would be waiting and hoping. Hoping for what? What had Nicodemus wanted to know? What had Jesus hoped he would ask?

Nicodemus spoke of eternal life by believing in Jesus, but there was no such thing. Life was measured in months and years, as grain was measured in omers and bushels.

Life was here and now with a vast storehouse of tomorrows for some. Yet death was here too—in the old who died, the young who never grew up, and those who were swept into the black abyss by accident or disease.

Death was a part of life. Life, indeed, proceeded from death. Nicolaus had tried to explain it. In death, other things could find life. In a dead dog, the flies laid eggs and were bred and fed. In the dead corn, the life seed sprang into green blades. From the loins of men who were now dead, many living walked the earth.

Life and death were inseparable, but death was always the victor. For all flies died, all corn was plucked, and all men turned to dust.

The cart wheels had been whining for many minutes before they became aware of them. John's garment was wet across his back.

The boy ran forward. "Let me pull awhile."

Joseph said, "I will relieve you, John."

But John said, "No. This I wish to do. Did He not wash my feet last night? Peter would have argued with Him but . . ."

Again the name of Peter struck the boy's mind, and he read in it a depth of sorrow, of disappointment.

"We must pray for Peter," Joseph said softly.

Nicodemus said, "It is hard for us to remember that one cannot rightly judge a day before the sun is set."

John spoke clearly, though he did not turn around or cease to pull the cart. "Last night, Nicodemus, as we shared the bread and wine, Jesus spoke many wonderful things. 'Let not your heart be troubled,' He said. 'Ye believe in God, believe also in Me. In My Father's house are many mansions. I go to prepare a place for you. And if I go, I will come again, and receive you unto Myself; that where I am, there ye may be also.'"

Vinegar Boy's heart leaped. Then Jesus *did* have a place where He could take Dysmas. Paradise must be the place of everlasting life. Thinking of the bright-haired Dysmas filled him with impatience to get back to the hill.

The cart was going so slow. How long had he been gone?

Would Jesus still be able to see, or hear, or speak?

"Please, please be all right," he whispered.

14
THE STORM

The cart with the aloes rumbled over the wooden ramp that crossed the highway gutter at the hill. A short distance beyond, the path that led to the burial garden turned left and wound through an avenue of tall cypress trees. At this point, John stopped the cart.

Joseph turned to Vinegar Boy and said, "God bless you for what you have done."

And the words of Nicodemus were like a benediction. "May the peace of God be with you now and forever." Vinegar Boy bowed to the masters of Israel. He felt awkward and a little foolish, but it seemed the proper thing to do.

Then John thrust out his hand, and the boy's fingers were lost in the nest of calluses. The fisherman's gaze swept the horizon. "When you get to the hill, tell my mother to come down to the garden. Have her fetch the other women, and tell her to come straightaway. There is going to be a storm."

Vinegar Boy looked up in disbelief. The sun blazed;

there were few clouds except over Mount Hermon. "Take my word," John said. "I can smell a storm. This could be a bad one."

Joseph and Nicodemus moved away. The small man walked with his hands behind him; Joseph swung his arms in wide, free gestures.

"What should we do with the cart, boy?" John asked. "I can return it to the commissary after the Sabbath."

"Leave it at the tomb, sir. I'll take care of it." Vinegar Boy raised his amber eyes to the fisherman. "I'm sorry about Jesus, sir. Tell His mother that I . . . liked her." He could feel his cheeks beginning to burn. The fire on the dark side was exceedingly hot.

But John's blue eyes appraised him affectionately. A smile of rare beauty broke on the fisherman's face. "She liked you too. The people in the house in the village are friends who can tell you where to find me if you ever need a favor." John's eyes lifted toward the hill. "I am sure that He knows you have helped us, and He has said that a cup of water given in His name shall have its reward. Tell your captain that I will come for the body as soon as I can."

"Why did they kill Him, sir?"

"I do not understand all of it myself. But someday I will. Then I will write it down so that other people will know. Yet, if I wrote down all that He has said and done, I doubt if the world itself would hold the books." Again the smile, slight but brilliant, touched the fisherman's face.

Over the noise of the cart on the gravel path, he turned and called back to the boy, "Remember. Tell the women to come straightaway."

"I will fetch them," Vinegar Boy yelled and waved

as he watched John disappear into the shadows of the cypress.

The pain of the blisters had doubled. The boy had tried not to limp in front of John, but now, as he climbed, he winced and groaned.

A small eddy of dust rose and hit him in the face. He lifted his hot face. The wind was rising a little, and a very light froth of clouds could be seen rising above the hills. Some of the brilliance of the blue sky was fading, and the Jordan Valley seemed to be filling with a copperish haze. If the wind continued it might bring sand, for often the gales picked up the sand in the desert places beyond the Jordan River, from beyond the wilderness of Moab.

In the stone corral at the foot of the cliff, the centurion's stallion neighed loudly. Vinegar Boy remembered that Rubicon was afraid of thunder, and incredible as it seemed, thunder had begun a low muttering in the east.

The thunder and the rising wind were driving a few of the lingering spectators from the hill. As they hurried past him, some of them were worrying about their gardens. If the rain came heavy and hard, they would have much of the seeding and planting to do over again. He thought of the hop plants he and Amoz, the garden overseer, had planted so carefully this week—more than two hundred of the little shoots in the small hills.

A hard rain would ruin the new hop field too. But surely this would not be such a storm. The rain would come, and the ground would soak up the water and be dry again by the time he went back to the city.

He would go back as soon as he had spoken to Jesus.

The first one he looked for as he reached the stony arena was Jesus. The Nazarene hung with His head down, His hair covering His face as though he had not moved in all the time the boy had been absent from the hill. The two outlaws hung equally quiet.

He looked for the women. They were still under the ancient tree. He started through the boulders toward them, but Marconius hailed him from the doorway of the shed. One leg was propped behind him, and his left hand pressed against the opposite doorpost. From where he stood the whole hill was under his surveillance.

Arno and Cloticus were the only soldiers the centurion had ordered to stay on the hill. They were playing knucklebones on the old door-table. The two playing pieces had been carved from some of the sandstone rocks of the hill. Just as the boy drew near, a gust of wind drove dirt and sand into Cloticus's face, causing him to make a wild throw. The knucklebones bounced from the door. One landed near the boy, and he picked it up, but the second was lost among the stones.

Cloticus cursed roundly. Arno laughed,

"Fifty *cesterces* you owe me already, Cloticus. The wind must be a friend of yours."

"The gods have deserted me. Fifty *cesterces*," Cloticus growled, "and no way to recoup my loss." He groaned.

Vinegar Boy tossed him the playing piece, and he caught it. Then he dropped it under his foot and crushed it. "Today is not my day," he growled again. "Even the dice left me without gain."

He spoke of Jesus' robe that Marconius had reserved for Mary.

Marconius didn't smile. "You're a bad loser, Cloticus. Perhaps you're hungry. Get your lunch and then go down to the corral. Stay with my horse until the threat of storm is over."

A long, low roll of thunder sounded. The stallion whinnied anxiously.

"I don't think the storm is going to blow over," Vinegar Boy said. "The fisherman John told me it might be a bad one. I didn't believe him but . . ."

The gray clouds that had been about the shoulders of Mount Hermon like a prayer shawl had raveled, portions of them floating toward the south. Lightning, like silver thread, wove in and out among them.

Marconius said, "I thought you were not coming back. You have been gone a long time. There has been no sound from Him."

"He isn't dead yet, is He?"

"No. But for His sake, I hope He goes quickly. I have no desire to break His bones."

"I would have been back sooner, but I had to go to the commissary for aloes." Quickly he told Marconius about John and Mary and the councilors.

"John wants the women to go down to the garden. I told him I would fetch them. When I come back—"

"We'll try to revive Him. He has had no vinegar." Marconius seemed worried. "I'm glad you are taking the women down; this is no place for someone who loves Him."

"Salome will probably go because John is her son, but the red-haired woman is stubborn, he said."

Marconius let his eyes stray to the tree. "Her spirit matches her hair."

His voice held admiration. He never spoke of women. Once, when Nicolaus had asked him about a wife, Marconius had said, "A soldier is better off without a wife. When I go into battle I want no one to worry about but myself."

As Marconius looked toward the woman called Magdalene, the boy wondered if the centurion might be changing his mind. He glanced up at Marconius and then away. The soldier would not want anyone to know how gentle his face could be.

A stronger gust of wind came, casting dirt broadside across the hill. The clouds in the east were foaming and rolling like froth on Roman beer. Lightning slashed the clouds, and claps of thunder echoed in the valley. The cry of the horse rose high and lonesome.

Marconius roared for Cloticus. "Finish your wine and get down the hill."

The legionary came out of the shed, wiping his mouth with his hand and holding a hunk of bread that dripped with curds of cheese. He was trying to fasten his helmet with one hand. As he passed the centurion, he snapped to attention.

Arno came to the doorway. "Should I check the supporting irons of the crosses, sir?"

"Yes. The storm might be over quickly, but one never knows." Marconius turned to Vinegar Boy. "Now let us get your friends away."

They were past the boulders of the amphitheater and heading for the old tree when the boy pointed beyond the edge of the cliff toward the south. A large, yellow cloud was rushing upward through the valley toward them. It came swiftly, blotting out everything in its path, with the frightening sound of rushing water.

Marconius yelled at the women, "Cover up!" And then the centurion grabbed the boy and swung him about. He pressed his face against him and tried to cover them both with his cloak. The cloud, laden with desert sand, hit in force. Under the cloak the boy choked and gasped. The sand cut his legs. The wind shook the timbers of the shed. The crosses creaked. The horses and the women screamed. When the air cleared, Magdalene was trying to stand; the other two women huddled like black toadstools beneath the tree. The wind had loosened Magdalene's hair and it glowed like flame against the gray sky.

Marconius stared. "Never in all my life—"

But the boy broke loose and ran toward the tree. "Salome! Salome!" he yelled. "John wants you to come down to the garden."

Salome leaned into the wind trying to hear. Magdalene heard. "No, we will not leave. John should be up here with us."

"He says there is going to be a very bad storm."

"No. Salome, you can't go." She grabbed at the older woman's arm. "We cannot leave Him alone."

"John wants all of you to come. Straightaway, he said." The boy was urgent.

"No!" Magdalene screamed. "You cannot leave our Lord."

Salome put her free arm about the smaller woman. "I must do what John says. Come, Mary."

"I will not go. I will not!"

"Stay, then," Salome said without anger, "but we are going." The other woman went without argument.

"Go!" Magdalene shrieked. The wind lifted her words and threw them back at her. "Be like all the others. Leave Him to die alone like a fox in the field!"

Vinegar Boy watched wide-eyed as lightning cracked the walls of heaven. Straight up and down from the center of the vault above them to the valley floor below the lightning glowed as the sunlight had glowed through the crack in the walls of the alley.

Behind the lightning the thunder came in a deafening blast. The hill trembled. Rubicon, the centurion's horse, screamed. The old tree bent in agony like a woman caught in the pangs of birth. A branch whipped loose and struck Magdalene across the shoulders. As if the branch had been a whip used on a stubborn child, she gathered up her skirts and ran after Salome. She stopped once, with the wind pushing her relentlessly, and threw a look at Jesus. Then the wind seemed to lift her from her feet and shove her on.

Large drops of rain splattered the stones. Faster and harder the rain came as the boy raced behind the women, urging them on. Hummocks of grass on the dirt path became treacherously slippery. The wind shoved and pushed them faster than their feet could go. The sun had been wiped out. Lightning continued to rip the covering of the sky.

Vinegar Boy tried to steady first one and then the other of the women. The small woman was light and swift on her feet like a young girl.

Their garments were soaking wet before they reached the bottom of the hill. The boy pointed to the cypress trees as they twisted and turned like ghostly shadows in the sweeping rain. "There—through there. There is a tomb in the cliff you can take shelter in."

At the end of the avenue of trees, the boy thought he saw someone coming. It must be John. Then Salome caught sight of him and began to call his name. Magdalene threw one look back over her shoulder at the boy, Her face was white, her eyes dark under the rain.

He waited only until he saw them reach John and the edge of the cypress, and then he turned back to the hill. He fought wind and rain to the top. In places, the slight covering of clay had become too slippery for walking, so he crawled, pulling himself up by the tufts of grass and bushes. His garment was sodden with mud. He took off his boots, his fingernails breaking as he tried to untie the wet laces. Resisting an impulse to throw the boots away, he hung them about his neck. The bandage on his arm came loose, and he dropped it in the mud. The wet clay helped to extinguish the pain in his toes and heels.

The wind battered his face and chest. It seemed to him that the world was displeased with him, although he did not know why. What had he done? This was supposed to be *his* day, and the whole morning was gone, and what had he gained? Nothing.

Tonight Phineas would laugh his ugly eyes out. Sparrow would chirp with sympathy. Nicolaus would be disappointed. No matter what he said, any man would prefer a son without an affliction.

And Jesus, the only Man in the whole world who could help him, was hanging unconscious on a cross, dying.

The wind was turning cold, and he shivered. But the chill brought a new hope. Perhaps under the rain and the coldness the Nazarene would revive.

Perhaps.

The hope began to move again deep within him, quivering like a newly hatched birdling.

He got to the top of the hill and lay panting. Through the gusts of driving rain he could see Jesus lolling on the upright. There was a laxness about the body that brought him to his feet. He stumbled forward. "No!" he cried. "No! You mustn't be dead. Not yet."

It seemed to him that there was no one left on the hill but himself and Jesus. Marconius and Arno had taken shelter in the shed, and the thieves hung silent.

He moved close to Jesus, his eyes fixed on His face. There was no sign of life. Then he saw the fingers move, opening and closing, stretching as if to touch the heads of the spikes that held His wrists.

Jesus was not dead. His hands were not dead, and it was His hands that did the healing.

Vinegar Boy pressed closer. Wind and rain wrestled with him, but he would not give up. He butted into the belly of the wind as he had butted into Phineas, and the wind gave way. Stumbling against the timber, he held fast. His hands touched the nailed feet, cold and smooth under the driving rain. The pelting drops cut his eyeballs, but he held his eyes on the face of the Man above him.

Words formed into a petition, silent and painful inside him. *Jesus! Lord! King!*

He struggled to speak and struggled again, but his lips would not open. The hope, fluttering like a wounded bird, fought to live. Surely Jesus would *know*. He *had* to know!

The feet convulsed beneath his hands. Jesus was pushing Himself upward for air. He was going to answer.

Now, Lord, please.

The lightning bolt struck so close that the acrid smell burned in the boy's nostrils. Behind the thunder, as it echoed on all sides of the hill, he heard Marconius shouting, "Get down, boy. Get down!"

He threw himself down. The wind caught him and rolled him like an empty cask until he came to rest against a boulder. Grabbing it with both hands, he pressed one foot hard against the other. The wind whipped and howled and pulled. Stones and dust cut his flesh and blinded him.

The fury of the gale came with the sound of a thousand racing chariots across the Jordan plains. The screams of the dying orchards and groves were like those of living things. The roof of the shed tore loose. Then the grasping fingers of the storm picked up the old door and sent it over the side of the cliff, and Vinegar Boy heard it strike far below. Above the wail of the wind, the death scream of the stallion was heard.

The old yew gave up its hold on the hillside and, after decades of victory over the storms, went down to defeat on the rocks below.

In the south, the wind swept across Jerusalem like an army of barbarians, with rain pouring its fury over walls and terraces. Dried bricks disintegrated, and homes collapsed. Sewers and gutters overflowed, and children climbed to tabletops to escape the swimming rats.

Behind the boy, a portion of the hill gave way over the corral, and mud and boulders poured down the abyss.

In the constant flashes of lightning, he saw that the farthest cross had tilted grotesquely. Dysmas groaned as his cross swayed. No sound came from Jesus. All the forces of the storm combined to assault the middle cross, but it held firm, as if a hand from heaven came down and held it steady.

Time and again the boy's eyes squinted shut against the terrifying display of lightning. Fireballs passed over and around the hill as it slung from a thousand slings. Bolts of lightning catapulted their firebrands against the hill.

Any fear Vinegar Boy had felt was forgotten as he watched the wrath of the storm. His head was up, his eyes open, when it happened. Marconius saw it, too, for he had been in the doorway of the roofless shed, held—even as the boy had been held—by the awesome display.

A tongue of fire struck, coiling and twisting like an angry serpent to wrap itself about the middle cross.

The boy cried out in horror. This was the end of Jesus.

Then the darkness fell, as if the Serpent—like an

ancient monster—had swallowed the light. Layer after layer of suffocating blackness came. The very atmosphere had a weight about it that stifled the wind. The world seemed to reel in amazement as if it had been cast back into the void from which the creation had lifted it.

In the midst of the terrifying, heavy silence, Jesus spoke in a voice that was not weak, but pitiful. Like the voice of a child who bas been shut away into a closet for a deed of mischief.

Vinegar Boy remembered the day Phineas had punished him in such a way. He remembered how frightened he had been, and how his cry had brought Nicolaus running to comfort him.

Now the voice of Jesus came from the darkness, calling His Father. "My God, my God, why hast Thou forsaken Me?"

Vinegar Boy waited. Waited for the blackness of the closet to give way to light. Waited for God to open the closed door and comfort His Son. But there was no word of comfort, no ray of light.

15
IT IS FINISHED

How long he sat in the unnatural darkness with his legs cramping from the cold, Vinegar Boy could never say. He tried to bring warmth back into his arms and legs by rubbing them. His back pressed hard against one of the boulders that had saved him from being blown from the hill.

There was no sound in the blackness as he tried to stand. The first tremors of the earth seemed no more than the weakness of his legs.

Later, when he and Marconius tried to tell about the strange darkness that fell at noonday and the earthquake that came, they were both uncertain about the length of time between one and the other. All they remembered was the violence and the terror.

The quivering and the trembling were more than the weakness of his own knees. Vinegar Boy put out his hand to balance himself against the boulder, and the stone was quivering. Feeling the increasing undulations beneath his feet, terror overcame him. He screamed for Marconius. As the centurion appeared out of the darkness, Vinegar Boy rushed toward him, grabbing at him, his fingers slipping on the cold, wet metal of the breastplate.

The centurion had just time enough to grab the boy before the sickness that had been gathering in the bowels of the earth exploded. Wave after wave of nausea convulsed the hill, and both of them were thrown from their feet. They lost their hold on each other, and Vinegar Boy could feel himself sliding downward. He screamed and grabbed at boulders that sprang from beneath his hands like live fowl.

Sensing that somewhere ahead of him there was a strip of nothingness, he screamed again. A burning brand caught him about the ankle as the rift closed with a snapping sound that shot rocks and dust into the air like a fountain.

Marconius hung on, his fingers digging into the boy's ankle. The spasms of the earth ceased as suddenly as they had begun.

Some bit of fire, struck by the lightning, had finished with secrecy and burst into voracious flame in the timbers of the old shed. The flames thrust through the smothering darkness like bright swords that bent and broke against the blackness.

Smoke rolled close to the ground, and the boy began to cough. Marconius picked him up and led him to the fire. He was shivering from cold and shock.

Somewhere to the west a viaduct had broken, and the waters were pouring like a waterfall.

The centurion looked about him with a mixture of awe and contemplation.

"Surely it must be over," he said. "The gods have nothing left to throw against us."

The scarlet cloak had been ripped from the Roman's back, and the larger part of it lay in a sodden heap by the burning timbers. He spread it for Vinegar Boy to sit on, and though it steamed and stunk in the heat of the fire, he was thankful for it.

Arno, the Syrian, came out of the shadows of the crucifixion arena, and Vinegar Boy suddenly remembered that there were more on the hill than just he and the centurion.

Arno had lost his helmet. The tunic under his leather cuirass clung to his shivering thighs. His dark face was gray in the light of the fire, and confusion clouded his eyes. He wrapped his arms about himself and turned round and round before the dancing flames as if he were a piece of roasting mutton.

"I checked the crosses, sir. One is in need of bracing. If those fellows are alive through this, they should win their pardon."

The Syrian ran his hand through his hair. It was thick with dust and stood in points over his ears.

"Get yourself warmed," Marconius said, "and then see how it is with Cloticus. I'm going to search for the wineskin."

Marconius picked up a piece of burning wood and went slowly about the area of the shattered shed. The brand was almost consumed when he came back carrying a battered vinegar bottle, the reed with the sponge, and the lance.

Remembrance came back to the boy and he put his head between his knees, How long had it been since he had started from the commissary with the vinegar and the sponge?

And today was to be *his* day, the day of his miracle.

Arno, too, had noticed the things that Marconius had laid on the cloak.

"This has been no ordinary execution, Captain."

Marconius cupped his hands before the fire, as though gathering warmth. "From the midnight hour last night, I have been sure that we were actors in an incredible drama. But the unreal has become real. And the stupidity irrevocable."

Arno picked up a torch. "I'm going down the hill now, Captain."

"Take care. There will be no path."

"What do you think has happened to Cloticus?" Vinegar Boy asked. It was strange that they had not heard from him. Suddenly he remembered the thudding sound of the old door and the scream of the horse. Surely Marconius must know that Rubicon was dead. Did he think that Cloticus was dead too? He could not tell from looking at Marconius as he squatted by the fire, drying the plume of his helmet.

Then, so quickly that the boy was startled, the centurion sprang to his feet, his hand on his sword. Dropping one hand in a gesture of silence toward the boy, he peered sharply into the shadows.

Someone was climbing the hill on the far side where the rough brush and pasture grass covered the hillside, and below, tilled terraces had fallen away toward the garden of tombs.

Marconius moved quietly into the deeper shadows. And in that moment the boy thought of Barabbas.

Why hadn't he thought of Barabbas before? The darkness that had fallen at midday would fool the outlaw. He would think it was night. Perhaps he had grown tired of waiting and had decided to make his way out of the city under cover of the storm.

Or maybe it wasn't Barabbas at all. Maybe Barabbas had died in the earthquake. Those old houses would have been the first to fall, and the rotten steps would be gone too.

But if Barabbas had escaped from Jerusalem, why would he come to the hill? Surely he wasn't foolish enough to think he could do anything about Dysmas.

Dysmas didn't have to be buried properly. Hadn't the outlaw understood about paradise? Didn't Barabbas know that paradise was better than a mountain pool where the sunset made rainbows in the falls?

Had Barabbas said something about a waterfall, or was he just imagining it? Maybe the broken viaduct and the sound of the water had made him imagine a waterfall. He was having a hard time sorting out the real things from the make-believe.

One thing was clear enough: Someone was coming, and Marconius was ready for him.

The voice sounded before the figure was plain.

"Captain?" The voice was resonant and peaceful.

Vinegar Boy felt his heart jump with relief. It wasn't Barabbas. It was John. "Marconius, it's the fisherman. It's John."

The Galilean crossed the ring of boulders and came toward the fire, his hoisted garments dripping with water. His face showed strain, and his eyes were not as blue as they had been earlier in the day. A strange aroma was about him; the boy finally realized it was that of burial spices.

"I have come for His body—when it is ready."

How calmly he spoke! Marconius nodded. His voice had an element of sympathy that was not lost on the fisherman. "He was still alive at our last check, but surely it cannot be long. If you wish . . ." He picked up another burning timber, and they went together. Vinegar Boy followed them, shivering as he left the fire. The stones of the bill seemed sharper under his feet since the storm had washed the sand away. He began to wonder where his boots could be.

None of the crucified men were dead. Dysmas opened his eyes, his head turning slowly to follow the flame of the torch. Jesus hung in silence. As the light crawled up His body, they could see the slight rise and fall of His extended ribs. His skin was blue, and muscles in His stomach moved like ripples on a stagnant pond.

The murderer hung at an angle. Marconius thrust the torch at Vinegar Boy and tried to raise the cross back to position. John helped him. They braced it with stones and then came back to the fire.

John squatted. Vinegar Boy wondered how often he had sat like that on the seashore eating fish from the luncheon fire or waiting for the other fishermen to come in with their boats.

"The boy has told you that we have permission to take Him?"

"Yes. But I have heard nothing from the governor."

"You will," John said. "My friends have gone back into the city to see to it."

"It's all right," Vinegar Boy said. "Pilate gave me the aloes after I reminded him that he had told Joseph he could have Jesus after He was dead."

"If He is not dead by sunset . . ." Marconius paused. John knew what he hesitated to say.

"He will be. There is a prophecy in our Scriptures, Captain, that tells us that not a bone of Him shall be broken."

Arno came out of the darkness behind him. Marconius looked up quickly and read the message on the Syrian's face.

"A rock slide got him, Captain. I saw his arm. There is nothing we can do."

Marconius brushed his hand across his lips. "He was a good soldier. But he was right—the gods were not with him today."

John laid his hand across the boy's knee. "Thank you for bringing my mother down. The garden was fairly destroyed, but we were safe in the tomb."

"The red-haired woman—who is she?" The centurion spoke almost abruptly in an attempt to be casual.

John looked at Marconius, and the boy saw what John saw. The gentleness and the interest were there, but Marconius did not realize it.

"Mary of Magdala. She is faithful to Him with good cause. He healed her of numerous afflictions—likened to the fury of seven devils."

"He has done nothing to kill her spirit."

John smiled. "No, He has only cleansed her."

"He blessed her too," Vinegar Boy said. "I saw Him. He promised her something wonderful, and she didn't even have to ask."

He told them of the thing he had seen in Jesus' face. Silence fell. The centurion broke it. "Tell me," he said. "Who is He, John? Why has this thing happened?"

As though the simple question turned a spigot, John's words began to pour out, sparkling and bright. Like white wine, they were in the darkness, mixed with spices to warm and comfort the heart.

"In Him, we have seen God. It is as though the Word of God became flesh and came to dwell with us."

John spoke slowly, as if he put words together in a way that he would remember later. "We beheld His glory, the glory as of the only begotten of the Father. He was full of grace and truth."

Vinegar boy listened and tried to decide why he liked John's voice so well. He was a Galilean and a fisherman, but he must have read poetry as Marconius did because he could speak like the Roman spoke. And the things that he talked about seemed to be happening right before their eyes.

"He came unto His own, but His own wanted none of Him. But to those who accepted Him, He gave new life. He brought light to darkness. He told us that His enemies would scourge Him and He would be lifted up. As the serpent in the wilderness in the history of our people, Captain, He would be lifted up—"

"This serpent. Is it a myth?"

John shook his head. "As you know, our ancestors were slaves in Egypt centuries ago. We have a history of being slaves, and we have a heritage of promised kingdoms. God sent us a leader to take our people out of bondage. But, as they went, they murmured and rebelled. Then judgment came upon them. Poisonous serpents afflicted the people, and they were bitten and died. But God did not leave us without hope. He instructed Moses to fashion a brazen serpent and hang it upon a pole in the midst of the camp. Those who looked upon the serpent that was lifted up would be saved."

John's voice faded, and his head turned toward the crosses.

"The serpent healed them?" Marconius sat with his chin against his chest, and his voice was muffled.

"No," John said. "Their faith in the promise of God saved them."

Vinegar Boy looked into the fire, and a copper flame lifted and twisted, reminding him of the lightning that had coiled like a great serpent about the middle cross. He must tell John about it.

"Did everyone have such faith?" Marconius asked. This time his head was lifted, and his eyes held those of John.

The fisherman shook his head. "Some thought it foolishness."

Arno had been forgotten in the discussion, but now he leaned forward. "If this Jesus is indeed your

Messiah, why did He not gather a force of men and drive us into the desert?"

"He did not come to destroy but to fulfill the word of God. He came to give His life a ransom for many. But it will not end here. No . . ." John leaned forward and stirred the edges of the fire, and a dying coal burst into renewed flames. "It will not end here. He has promised that He will come again and receive us unto Himself."

In the silence that followed the amazing words, there was a stirring on the middle cross. The sound brought all of them to attention. Vinegar Boy went forward. If Jesus had been clothed in light and ready to step down from the cross with a crown on His head, he would not have been surprised.

But there was no light—only the cry of a torment-ed Man. "I thirst."

John looked around. "Water!" he said to Arno. Marconius grabbed up the vinegar bottle.

"The sponge," the boy reminded him.

They filled the sponge, and it was Arno who raised it to the dying Man's lips. Jesus sucked slowly as His eyes roved over the faces of those below Him. Vinegar Boy saw His gaze stop on John. Then He turned His face away from the sponge, and He cried out in a voice that was startling in its strength.

"It is finished!"

The cry rebounded in the hollow darkness. It was a glad cry. A triumphant cry. The cry of a Man who had caught a glimpse of His Father's house after a long absence.

And as the words went forth, the veil of darkness split from north to south, east and west. The portions of black rolled back. The hill moved once beneath their feet as if to gain a permanent resting place.

For a moment it seemed that the air was filled with the echoes of the mocking voices that had been heard during the day.

The sun, brazen and full in the third hour of the afternoon, struck the face of Jesus. He was bathed in gold.

"Father!" The voice rang again, and light continued to shower upon the mutilated but radiant face. "Father, into Thy hands I commend My spirit."

A shudder passed through Him. A sigh rose, lingered on the air, and was gone. His head dropped.

Jesus of Nazareth was dead.

As simply as Vinegar Boy would have handed a tool to Nicolaus to mend, so Jesus breathed out His life into the keeping of His Father.

John sank to his knees, his blue eyes flooding.

Arno raised the lance. "We must be sure."

Marconius took the lance and moved toward the cross. Vinegar Boy shut his eyes. He heard the thrust.

Then Marconius said in a heavy voice, "Now it is indeed finished."

With the words, a strange thankfulness filled the boy. He did not understand why he should be glad that Jesus was dead. His heart should be shattered, for he had not received his healing.

He put his hand to his ugly cheek. He was surprised to find it wet with tears.

16
SUNSET

Dysmas, the young rebel, moaned. Hearing him, the boy looked up at the glazed eyes under the dull hair that had been bright as sunlight when the day started. The outlaw's tongue, raw and swollen, tried to get through his lips.

"Do you want a drink?"

The faintest shake of the head answered him.

"Jesus is dead," Vinegar Boy said. "But He is waiting for you wherever He is. You don't have to worry about anything anymore."

The fever-burned lips tried to smile. The boy shuddered. Dysmas took a deep breath and let his weight settle again. His face turned toward the sun. The boy could almost feel, on his own scalp, the fingers of the sun as they moved through the outlaw's drying hair.

Dysmas never opened his eyes again. Not even later when the executioner slipped the cold iron rod behind his legs and cracked the bones with the mallet.

Vinegar Boy could never remember when the executioner had returned to the hill. He could remember talking to Dysmas, but after that things became mixed up. He knew that John had gone from the hill to fetch help to get Jesus' body. And he knew that Marconius had sent Arno back to Jerusalem to carry word of the Nazarene's death and to check on the disposition of the body. If it was not Pilate's desire to have the Nazarene turned over to His friends, then Arno should send word by courier. Marconius would keep solitary watch on the hill until the leg-breaker came.

Vinegar Boy stood by himself at the corner of the hill where the deluge had left mud-filled caverns where the yew tree had been uprooted. His head felt strange, as if it weren't a head at all but a pig's bladder blown up and tied to his neck with string. He felt weightless, as if he could flap his arms and sail off the hill like a long-legged bird.

Valley and city swam before his eyes. He sat down quickly, and not a moment too soon. One minute more and he would have toppled into the water-filled holes or over the cliff to the rocks below.

What was the matter with him?

He held his eyes shut to keep the world from turning. When he opened them, he saw the executioner cleaning the gore from the bar and the mallet with a handful of cold ashes from the burned shed. The man was cursing under his breath. His hand had been too heavy—his judgment the worse for wine. He always prided himself on a clean job.

Vinegar Boy wondered which outlaw had the mangled legs. The big one, probably. Maybe the executioner had not forgotten the vinegar that had hit him in the face.

Vinegar Boy tried to think back, to sort out the different parts of the day as he would sort turnips or cabbages, but he could not. The hill seemed to be full of people again. The voices and the mockeries were being repeated all over again. "If He be the Christ, let Him come down from the cross, and we will believe Him." "He saved others, Himself He cannot save." He heard the cursings of the big outlaw, the groans of Dysmas, the weeping of Mary, and the accusations of the red-haired Magdalene. And he heard the wild cry of John Mark, "This is Jesus of Nazareth, the King of the Jews."

The cries crescendoed until he threw his hands over his ears and buried his face in his lap. Then the voices faded, and he knew that if he opened his eyes he would see the hill as it was. Opening them, he saw the executioner moving toward the middle cross. What was the matter with him? Didn't he know Jesus was dead?

He tried to rise, but the floating feeling came back, and he sat down again. What difference did it make? A dead man couldn't feel anything. Besides, Jesus wasn't there. He was in paradise.

But Marconius stopped the executioner with a bellow that could have been heard on the highway. "Leave the Nazarene alone. He is dead."

"How do I know unless I test them? You sure He's dead?"

Then he saw the lance hole, and he grunted half in apology, half disappointment. "Died pretty quick, didn't He? These preachers are weak fellows."

The executioner put the bar and mallet back into the leather pouch that hung over his shoulder. "The tribune says you are to wait until the last possible minute to put them out of their agony. In fact, he said to keep them alive until the sun gets its behind wet in the Great Sea," the leg-breaker chuckled.

Marconius squared his jaw. The boy, listening, felt a desire to giggle.

What was it the tribune had said? Something about the sun getting its—no, no, he mustn't giggle. Not here. Not now. Marconius wouldn't like it. Marconius was awfully serious right now—like an old man. He'd better not giggle. It might not come out a giggle. There might be a whole hill full of giggles jumping about like grasshoppers. He would laugh and laugh and never stop laughing.

He bit his lip and grabbed the earth. He must stop thinking. He should make his head empty—like an empty barrel. Real empty. So if anyone banged on it, all he'd get was a dull echo. He began to giggle. No, he mustn't giggle. He had better look at the sunset. Look at it until his eyes hurt.

He was sorry Dysmas wouldn't open his eyes. He didn't know how beautiful the sunset was. Pale green and rose and purple were wiped across the sky as if a child had emptied buckets of paint. The sun had started its descent after the third hour of darkness like a small, golden denarius rolling down the side of the sky. But now the sun was round and fat as a shield. Gloriously bright. So bright it hurt his eyes. He put his head on his knees and watched a whole lot of little suns go round and round and round.

He never knew if he fell asleep or not, but when he came to, the executioner was gone, and Marconius had administered the death thrusts, even though the sun had not touched the sea. The burial carts would come later with the lime buckets hanging on the side.

The bodies of the outlaws would be hauled away to the valley of Gehenna, where they would be sprinkled with lime and left to rot. Sometimes the bodies were thrown on the refuse fires.

He wished he could do something for Dysmas. Barabbas had wanted him to do something, but what could he do?

He stood up, every muscle of his body aching. The pain of his bleeding feet had long since disappeared in a host of other pains. Nicolaus would bathe and salve and scold. How good it would be to have a bath and crawl under the clean blankets of his bed. The moonlight would pour through the shutters, and Sparrow would rouse in the eaves and chirp a sleepy welcome.

Slowly he moved toward the cross on which Dysmas hung. Yes, the smile was still on the swollen lips. Vinegar Boy laid his head against the upright. "Where are you? Are you with Jesus?"

The dizziness was returning. It seemed the hill rolled under his feet like waves of an ocean. He felt no urge to scream. He would stand like John and let the waves get higher and higher and—

Marconius came toward him but stopped in front of the middle cross. The boy noticed with surprise that Jesus was gone. When had John taken the body?

The centurion's cheeks were dark with beard. Sweat and dirt made the ringlets of his black hair stiff across his forehead. He carried his helmet. The black plume was ruined. He laid the helmet at the foot of the empty cross. Then he took off the sword belt and laid it with the helmet. He moved and spoke as if he were the only one on the hill.

Vinegar Boy clung to the other cross and listened.

Marconius looked up. The rough-hewn beam pointed like a black finger against the sky. Rays from the setting sun shot sparks from the nails that had held the title board. The sign had been blown away in the storm, but it seemed that Marconius was reading it.

"This is Jesus of Nazareth, the King of the Jews."

He spoke softly but clearly. "Sir, I stand before You without helmet, cloak, or sword. And I say unto You, where is my authority? What have I within myself that makes me a commander of men? But You, Sir, You wore no helmet and no sword, and yet You were the Master of all. You could have said to the wind, 'Go,' and it would have gone. To the lightning, 'Come,' and it would have consumed us.

"I have seen men go willingly and obediently to their death. But death is Your servant. He came as You commanded.

"Jesus of Nazareth, behold me. I too wish to be remembered when You come in Your kingdom."

Marconius knelt on both knees. "Lord, be merciful to me, for truly You were the Son of God."

The lightness left the boy's head. A feeling of sympathy took him on the run to Marconius.

The centurion still knelt with one knee lifted, his fists doubled under his chin as he wept.

"Don't cry, Marconius. He heard you. Don't cry."

The crunch of gravel behind them made the boy look up. His amber eyes, tired and dull, blazed in surprise. His lips opened in a cry of amazement. "Barabbas!"

Marconius swung about. His hand scooped up the sword, and he turned, crouching. Tears made his eyes shimmer under the setting sun, but the deadly intent behind them was plain to see. Suddenly, incomprehensibly to the boy, Marconius had become Rome again. Bloody, killing Rome.

The sword would have lodged itself in Barabbas's exhausted body if Vinegar Boy had not thrown himself against the springing centurion. Marconius, taken entirely by surprise, sprawled on his back. The sword spun out of reach. Vinegar Boy stood over him, his whole body trembling.

"You can't kill him! He's free! Jesus died in his place." Then the young voice rose. "Haven't you killed enough for one day?'

The birthmark stood out in the golden light. The boy's tired, hungry, dirty body went limp. His head pitched forward, then his body. He catapulted into the Roman's lap. Under the weight of the boy, with the sword lying between them, there would have been no chance for Marconius if Barabbas had decided to strike. The knowledge was there in the flashing of eyes. Then Barabbas kicked the sword away and knelt to lift the boy. The hands of the enemies met beneath his body. Their eyes met across his pitiful, beautiful face.

Barabbas took a slow, deep breath and said, "I owe him my life. He found me in an alley where I dragged myself after your men threw me out last night. He brought me bread and water. He was going to take me out of the city tonight, but the earthquake forced me to take my own chances. The darkness in the city was a gift of God. The quake might well have finished me, except it has become clear to me that this is not the day for Barabbas to die."

"I would have killed you," Marconius confessed quietly. "But he is right. I have no reason to collect a debt that has already been paid."

Marconius began to slap the boy's dark cheek. Barabbas picked up the boy's dirty, bruised hands and rubbed them gently between his own. He showed the blisters to Marconius, and the centurion nodded. "He hauled a cart of aloes . . ."

The centurion shifted to a sitting position, and the boy's eyes fluttered. He heard them talking, but he kept his eyelids shut.

Marconius said, "As the cross is my witness, you need have no fear of me."

Barabbas answered softly, "Neither have I a desire to do you evil. This is a strange thing, for this morning I would have damned the host of you to hell."

The boy moved and opened his eyes. He was not dreaming. Close above him, both with the same anxious looks upon their faces, he saw the mortal enemies. Something had changed them. What?

He heard Barabbas talking softly. "What kind of Man died on that middle cross, Centurion? For a good man, one might die, but scarcely for a wicked man. Why did they crucify Him and let me go? Even in the dungeon it was said that Pilate found no fault with Him."

Marconius answered. The boy was glad that he was listening with his eyes closed tightly again. The words were wonderful enough. They were the kind of words John would use.

"You know the laws of your Mosaic sacrifices?"

"As well as most. Of late I have been too busy to observe the washing of the inside of the platters."

Marconius must be smiling slightly. The smile was in his speech. "In all religions there are such things that one fails to observe. But in the one essential thing, your people have been faithful. They believe that God meets with them in the blood atonement, is that not so?"

"Our Scripture makes it plain. It is the blood that makes atonement for the soul."

"Then listen. Consider what I say. I believe that to-day, at the time of your own holy preparations, Jesus of Nazareth died for the sins of men as the Lamb of God."

Vinegar Boy's eyes flew open. He saw the look of

dawning comprehension on the outlaw's beaten face. "If that is so, then I—I, Barabbas—am as the scapegoat. It is written in the same book of the law that the high priest shall have the congregation cast lots for the goats—one goat for the sin offering, one for the scapegoat. The sin offering is slain; the scapegoat goes free."

Barabbas hesitated. Then he added, "There are those among our teachers who have believed that our Messiah would come first, not as a monarch, but as a servant. He would bear our iniquities, and we would find healing in His stripes."

The word *stripes* hung like a pall between them for a moment. Barabbas had found a workman's cloak, but it could not completely conceal the crusted, ugly wounds on his legs and chest.

He strode to the middle cross. "This is where my judgment was completed. He died in my place. I cannot explain it, Centurion, but it is as though the old hawk has grown new feathers."

Marconius put out his hand, and Barabbas gripped it. There was a glow of happiness about them that the boy could not understand. Later he would become familiar with the glow and would feel his own heart warmed and lifted.

"Barabbas," he said, "why did you come up here? Why didn't you go to the hills?"

Barabbas came back and squatted beside him. "I don't really know, boy. It had something do with you, and a promise that I had made to someone I loved as your steward loves you." Barabbas looked up at Marconius. "I seek a favor. I would like to have the body of Dysmas. He was my friend."

Marconius said, "Take him. I may have to answer for it to the tribune, but take him. He died well."

"You'll need some help," Vinegar Boy said. He tried to stand. He staggered with weakness, and Barabbas steadied him. "Could he use the commissary cart, Marconius? It will hold Dysmas. I will fetch it."

He started forward, and Marconius leaped toward him, for the boy swayed. "We will fetch it together. You have done all that you are going to do for anyone today."

The garden was silent and still as they entered it. The odor of embalming spices clung about the tomb. A stone had been rolled across its entrance, but there was no permanent seal. Perhaps there was something yet to be done.

The cart was there. Marconius lifted the boy into it. "You're going to ride, boy." The feel of his arms made Vinegar Boy lonesome for Nicolaus. He hunched his knees under his chin, and his hips took the jolting as the cart bounced over the ruts and gullies.

Behind him, the face of the cliff disappeared into the evening shadows. Overhead the colors of the sunset ran outward, growing progressively paler until they reached the eastern horizon. All the colors of the weaver's dyeing vats had been emptied across the sky.

Crimson and purple, gray and gold, violet and blue, yellow and green. The colors of the day. He tried to sort them out. Violet for Mary's eyes; scarlet for the centurion's cloak; gold for the young thief's hair; purple for the stripes on Barabbas; green for the silk of Procula's gown. Blue? Blue for the eyes of John, of course.

Then, in a burst of glory, the sun fell like a ripe apricot into the sea, carrying the colors of the sunset with it. A lingering shaft of light hit the hill and loitered, as if reluctant to close the gate on that day. Above them, Barabbas worked to lower the body of his friend.

Vinegar Boy thought of his boots. He must find them. He called out to Marconius and told him so, and the centurion said they would. "But you rest now, do you hear?"

Vinegar Boy laid his face on his knees. He would put the boots in a chest in his room and would never wear them again. He slept soundly as the cart groaned up the hill.

He slept all the time Marconius carried him and his boots down the highway and through the city gates and into the garrison, where Nicolaus waited with his arms outstretched.

A little later, the steward and the centurion stood together beside the sagging shutter in the little attic room and whispered. "Tomorrow, what can I say to him, Marconius? How can I make him understand that I want to adopt him just as he is?"

"No man could have a better son. Tell him that I do not believe that the time of miracles is gone. I have the feeling we will see great and mysterious things in the next few days. Tell him I said so."

Nicolaus nodded. Marconius went down the steps, but the steward washed the dirt and the blood away. He eased the bruised body out of the ruined garment, and he wept when he saw the hands and the feet.

The boy murmured, and Nicolaus leaned near to hear. "I tried, Nicolaus. I tried. But I couldn't ask Him. I couldn't . . ." The sleepy voice failed.

"You shouldn't have had to ask Him, son." Nicolaus let his tears fall. The boy opened his eyes for a minute, trying to make Nicolaus understand. "He didn't have time, Nicolaus. He was busy doing an errand."

His voice trailed off, and he slept. The steward finished with the task of caring for him, and then he knelt at the window.

"Help me," he prayed. "Whoever You are, whatever You are, Jesus of Nazareth, my boy believed in You. Do not fail him. If You would have me, do not forget my son."

The boy moaned a little, and Nicolaus picked up his hand and held it close.

PART 2

DAYS OF GLADNESS

17
RESURRECTION DAY

Sparrow teetered on the window ledge outside the half-closed shutters and sang. It was the first day of the week, very early in the morning.

He is risen! He is risen!

Vinegar Boy rolled over on his pallet of blankets, opened his eyes, and stretched. He was still sore in spots, but the raw places on his heels and toes had dried and darkened until they looked like new copper coins against the tan of his feet.

He rose quickly and ran to the window. He had dreamed that Sparrow was singing out words to him as he slept. The shutter swung wide, and the bird hovered on whistling wings. The boy could feel the stir of happiness in the air. Sunlight danced on stone and beamed across the holy city.

"What is it, Sparrow? Why is the world so full of joy and gladness this morning?"

Sparrow fluttered, flipped, and floated. Over and around, off and on the window ledge he soared, riding the shutters as if he were a caged bird swinging in the gardens of the rich. In the nest in the eaves above him, his dark brown mate and the little ones with their featherless necks chirped in chorus.

He is risen! He is risen!

Vinegar Boy leaned out of the window. He could not see field or garden. His eyes saw no green at all except a small, wooden tub of geraniums under the arches of the barracks, where a homesick recruit had planted flowers such as had grown in his mother's garden.

The very air was filled with music. The song of rejoicing came from the cucumber patches with their running vines and from the onion beds with their dancing stalks, from the hop fields where the new cuttings were taking root after the storm had washed out the first planting.

The music came from the olive groves and the orchards, from the pomegranate trees and the flowering apricots, from the wild roses in the flax fields and the lilies blooming amid the tall grass of the wayside.

What was the message of the song?

He is risen! He is risen!

The sunlight warmed the boy's body, and his whole being throbbed in answer to the song he could not understand.

Surely, surely the hills about Jerusalem were skipping like little lambs, and the trees of the forests were clapping their hands in joy.

From behind him came the sound of running feet. Someone was taking the stone stairs two steps at a time. Marconius burst into the room, wearing only short trousers and a military tunic. His black hair curled about his forehead. He had not yet shaved, and his face, what part was not shining with jubilance, was dark with beard.

Behind him, Nicolaus climbed more slowly, breathing

hard. He watched as Marconius grabbed the boy and swung him high.

"He has risen, boy! He has risen!"

The words fit Sparrow's song, and the boy suddenly knew why the earth was bursting with gladness. Jesus of Nazareth had risen! Risen from the dead!

"Come on, get dressed," Marconius said. "We're going to the garden to see for ourselves if the story the guards are telling is true."

"Oh, it is true!" Vinegar Boy said. "Can't you feel it? Even Sparrow knows it is true."

As Nicolaus helped Vinegar Boy dress, Marconius told them what he had heard. He told them of the uproar at the palace as Pilate interrogated the priests and the guards. He told of the panic in the courts of the Jewish rulers as the Sanhedrin showed signs of falling apart. Many of the councilors, like Joseph and Nicodemus, could no longer deny their faith in Jesus as the Messiah of Israel.

The boy fastened his sandals. The boots he had worn on the day of sadness had been laid away in the small chest that Nicolaus had made for him. The chest, made of cedar wood, stood near the window under the shelf where the bag of grain was kept.

But Marconius was going on. "The rulers are paying the guards to be silent about the truth. It is to be rumored that His friends stole the body away. But it is not so. I have questioned them. The detail that was ordered out to watch the tomb has come in. The men were white and shaken. Sight has not yet come back fully into their eyes. There was a light, fiercer than desert sunlight, sharper than a lightning flash, they said. And the stone in front of the tomb became as parchment, the seal as wax. Jesus came forth. No stripes upon Him. His beard full. His garments white—white as rain-cleansed clouds. And the earth shook as He came forth. The stone rolled back, and the light that surrounded Him conquered the darkness of the grave. The watchers admit they fell as dead men before His glory."

Nicolaus listened, his face serious but his blue eyes glowing. "You are certain it is the same Man who lives again?"

"He lives! He lives! I will take the boy with me to the garden. He deserves to see for himself."

"And then?" Nicolaus paused. A look passed between the two men.

"Then we will find Him," Marconius said.

A white Arabian mare, which Marconius had chosen after the death of the gray stallion, stood ready for them as they came out into the gentle light of dawn.

They passed from the city gates and broke into a canter. Three days before, the highway north had been a road of sorrow and sadness for the boy. Now the sun danced, trailing her morning scarves across the lawns and hedges. The air was fresh with flower scents. In the sky, the blue stretched and stretched as if there could be no end of blueness.

In the garden, beyond the dark cypress trees, the grave stood empty. Vinegar Boy did not enter the tomb, but Marconius did. The boy stood with his hand on the large, round stone that had sealed the grave. The sunlight had warmed it, and it seemed to him that the stone was vibrating with humming.

Marconius came back into the sunlight, blinking. "The clothes are there that they wound Him in. And the napkin that they laid across His head is there. But He is not there. He has risen, as they said."

"Where is He, Marconius? Can we find Him?"

"We will try. And if we do, Nicolaus and I will see to it that you receive the favor you deserve."

The miracle? But he had given up all hopes of a miracle. Even now, when his heart should be jumping with excitement and hope, he was thinking more of Jesus than of his face.

"Where could Jesus be?"

"Maybe in the village, Marconius, in the little house with the garden where the fisherman took Mary. Perhaps they are still there."

"It is as good a place as any to begin," Marconius said, laying his heels to the flanks of the mare. The Arabian stretched out into a racing stride.

The village stood as cool and quiet as the boy remembered it. The bell on the gate tinkled merrily, but the garden was deserted. The door of the house was closed. Some of the wreckage from the storm had been swept up into piles near the grape arbor, but it had not been carried away. The poppies that had danced in a vivid pattern against the wall were ruined. The blooms lay dark and dead upon the ground.

As they left the garden, the boy turned and swung the bell. The melody set the birds to singing. "Listen. It is the song Sparrow sang. 'He is risen! He is risen!'"

Marconius did not laugh at his fancy. Just then an old man hobbled from the courtyard on the opposite side of the street

"If you are seeking the Galileans, they are not there. They have gone into the city, for they have heard that Jesus the Lord has risen."

"Where in the city?" Marconius asked.

"I do not know. It is a secret place. " Then the old man added, "How will they feel when He stands among them—those who failed Him, those who denied Him? Ah, that I were young and strong again and could serve such a Master."

"Where can we find Him?" Marconius insisted gently.

The old man leaned down and plucked a cluster of small, white flowers. Bell-shaped and fragrant, the blossoms swung on a slender stem between broad green leaves that shone in the sunlight as if they had been freshly oiled.

"For your mother," he told the boy. "Today should be a day of flowers for mothers in praise of the maiden who gave Him suck. Our Lord has conquered death, Centurion. And we who trust shall also rise. Is it not so?" There was no fear in the old man's face that spoke of death, although the boy knew that death could be only a few short steps away.

Marconius gripped the trembling hand. "It's true, old friend, it's true."

The wizened face squinted up at Marconius, and the boy wondered how the old man had known that he was a centurion. But the old were always wiser than the young.

"You are not an Israelite, my friend," the old man said. "And for a while it will be with you as with the sheep of another pasture, or the olives that grow wild outside the grove. But there will come a time when you will be accepted, when you shall be grafted to the stem of Jesse."

Vinegar Boy thought the old man was rambling, but Marconius listened closely with respect. "There is a sign in your Temple that says, 'This far and no farther for a Gentile,' but I have heard that He said that whosoever wished to come to Him would not be cast aside."

The old head bobbed. The shaking hand fell to his side. "Peace ride with you."

Marconius slapped the reins against the mare's neck, and they were off again.

Later, as they were entering the city, they passed a beggar woman. Marconius turned and spoke over his shoulder. "I came without my purse." But the boy nudged him to stop. He leaned over and pressed the white flower into the waiting hand. "We have no money, but here is a gift for you."

She muttered an imprecation under her breath. But as the fragrance of the flowers reached her, she lifted the cool cluster against her wrinkled cheek.

The boy smiled. "Have you heard? The Lord has risen!" A smile began on her witless face and gave her a touch of beauty. As the white mare moved on, the boy looked back. The fingers fondled the petals, and her eyes followed them. The smile was still there. He waved, then he said, "Marconius, we must begin to tell everyone that the Lord has risen."

The next day Marconius came to the commissary. "I have heard that Jesus intends to meet with His disciples and friends somewhere in Galilee. I intend to seek them out. Arno has taken command for the next month. I am going to find the Galileans, and then I will send for you."

"But, Marconius, I can't leave here and go into Galilee. The work in the hop fields is increasing."

"We will see about that," Nicolaus said. "If you find Him, Marconius, do you think there will be more miracles? Or will these days see the beginning of something new?"

"I don't know, Nicolaus. I am as a babe in the faith. But I intend to grow."

"But will they teach you?" Vinegar Boy asked. "The old man said—"

"That I am not of their pasture? That is so, but He who forgave His enemies and welcomed a thief into His kingdom will not turn His back on me. Neither will He forget what you have done for Him, boy. The way you helped His mother and the other women . . ."

And then Marconius told them of Magdalene. He had heard that it was the red-haired woman who had first beheld the risen Jesus.

"He appeared to her before any other. She came later with other women to the tomb, and they found two men in white, one sitting at the head, the other at the foot. And the men asked them why they were seeking Jesus among the dead. 'He is not here. He is risen,' they said."

As Marconius spoke, the boy could see the angels, and he suddenly knew that was the blessing that Jesus had bestowed upon the fiery Magdalene. She had seen Him first!

That evening the centurion hung his saddlebags across the white mare and departed from Jerusalem for Galilee. Vinegar Boy watched through tears as he went. Would Marconius return soon? Would he send back word concerning Jesus as he had promised?

Nicolaus put his arm about him and pressed him close. "He will return. He has promised to be a witness for us when we appear before the judge."

That was all Nicolaus said. It was the first time he had mentioned the adoption since the day of sadness. But the love and longing were there, and the boy knew that he could not deny Nicolaus any longer. He must choose a name. The birthmark was still there, but it did not bother him so much. When he felt sorry for himself, he thought of Jesus. He had been called worse names than "Liver Face," and yet He had continued to be kind.

As Vinegar Boy thought upon a name, he knew what name he wished to use, what kind of man he wished to be. But first he must ask the one who owned the name. A person didn't just borrow another man's name without asking.

18
DAY OF RECOMPENSE

Several days after the resurrection of Jesus, Nicode-mus came to the commissary to settle for the price of the aloes.

Vinegar Boy had been returning from the gardens with a bag of early peas when he saw the man with the billowing black-and-yellow robes asking directions from a porter near the palace gates.

He ran to tell Nicolaus, knowing the steward would want to take off his work apron and put on a clean cap.

Nicolaus greeted the councilor with dignity and honor. Vinegar Boy washed his face and hands, and poured the peas into a small basket. He sat cross-legged on the doorsill, with a pan for the shelled peas between his knees.

At first, as the councilor talked, Nicolaus shook his head stubbornly. "The aloes have already been put to my account."

But Nicodemus was fluent with words and hands. He *must* pay for the aloes, and Nicolaus must not deny him this chance to right a wrong. He had been afraid to confess his allegiance to the Nazarene. His voice went on, irresistibly persuasive. Finally Nicolaus threw up his heavy arms in surrender.

The boy grinned as the pods snapped and the peas rattled into the pan. Nicolaus had met his match in the "scholarly turtle."

Money passed from the councilor to Nicolaus. The steward went into the account room and came back with a proper receipt. Then, as they sat at the table, Nicolaus poured a cup of fine red wine, and Nicodemus spoke of Jesus as the Messiah of the Jews and the Savior of the world as he had told the boy he would do.

"Freedom, Steward? Even with your manumission papers you have not been free. What man is free until he is free of the penalty and burden of sin? Jesus told us, 'Whosoever commits sin is the servant of sin. If God's Son, therefore, shall make you free, you shall be free indeed.'"

Nicolaus listened because the councilor was saying things that the steward had always believed, and he was explaining them in terms that he understood.

"You, as an honest steward, must honor the drafts of the governor upon the supplies in your warehouse. So must the Father in heaven, henceforth, honor the faith of those who draw upon His mercies through the name of His Son."

"I have full intentions of believing, Councilor. But first God must show me that He intends to recompense my son. I have talked to Him about it. If He wishes to have my allegiance, He must do what is right for the boy."

Vinegar Boy, sitting quietly shelling peas, felt his face flaming. He had not known that Nicolaus had talked to God about him.

The sharp, black eyes of the councilor burned beneath their heavy lids. "Faith does not come in a barrel, Steward, to be opened when you please. You cannot weigh to yourself one portion of faith, great or small. Not so much as a grain of faith will come by a man's own will. Faith is a gift of God."

The peas fell quietly, a tiny green mountain forming in the bottom of the pan. A line of perspiration sat on the steward's forehead. He removed the cap.

"If you had seen the boy that night . . ." His big voice broke.

The councilor's black eyes shone clear and thin as candle tips. "He has already received a recompense, Steward. Have you not seen that for yourself?"

A pod broke sharply under the boy's thumb. What did Nicodemus mean?

"The mark no longer plagues him."

How did Nicodemus know? It was true. The birthmark was still there in all its purplish red ugliness, but it did not fill him with unhappiness anymore. Not even Phineas with his mocking tongue had been able to spoil his days of gladness since Jesus had risen.

When Nicodemus was gone, Vinegar Boy stood before Nicolaus with the pan of peas in his hands.

"I did not know that you had asked God for a miracle for me."

"What father does not desire the best for his son?"

"But I want you to believe in Jesus the way Marconius does, even if my cheek isn't changed."

The Gallic chin grew stubborn, the pale blue eyes determined.

"I have not minded the mark, boy, but you wish a new cheek. And I will serve no God who is not just and fair enough to see that you have it,"

Tears swam in the amber eyes. "If He comes back,

185

I will ask Him. I have not stopped *wanting* my face fixed, Nicolaus! It is just that the mark does not rub as a blister anymore. Nicodemus is right. I have received a miracle."

Nicolaus pulled the boy to his lap, and the pan of peas upset. They rolled across the floor. Later, as Phineas passed their door on his way to the meat larder, he saw the steward on his knees, playing marbles with the fresh green peas. The boy was opposite him, eagerly engaged in the game. Nicolaus was roaring in his big voice, "Knuckle down, boy. Quit hunching."

Vinegar Boy saw the shadow of Phineas upon the floor and looked up at him. "Peace to you, Phineas. The Lord is risen."

The butcher moved on, muttering to himself. The heavy door jarred shut behind him. Nicolaus sat back, breathing heavily.

"You will never see a change in that one."

"God can do it if He wants to."

"Not that one. He has a heart of stone."

The boy did not argue. Nicolaus might be right. Already it seemed that some would believe in Jesus and some would not, even though He had risen from the dead.

The next day the first of the reports came from Marconius in Galilee. A training unit of raw recruits who had been on field maneuvers brought it in. Marconius had located the main body of believers. He had talked to friends in Capernaum, where a fellow centurion was in the confidence of the Jews. Although he had not yet seen or heard Jesus, there was no doubt that others had.

The second note came a little later. Scribbled hurriedly, as if Marconius had written it on his knee, the message arrived with a donkey train delivering a shipment of embroidered cloth to the palace. Nicolaus and Vinegar Boy opened it together.

Marconius had seen Jesus. He had heard Him, even though he had stood afar off. From what he could gather, Jesus did not intend to remain in Galilee. He was planning to return to Bethany, but—and Marconius had underlined the words—*"He is not staying in Judea either. He is going to return to His Father in heaven.* If the boy wishes to see Him, he must be in Bethany when the Galileans get there. Rumors are in conflict. I will let you know exactly when to look for Him, if possible. Keep your ears open, boy. Be watchful of the Bethany road as you work in the fields. There have been no reports of miracles."

As they read the note, Vinegar Boy exclaimed, "Jesus is coming back!"

But Nicolaus said, "You have one more chance, boy. You must not let it slip through your fingers like a ripened barley grain."

"I won't, Nicolaus. I won't." His amber eyes glowed, not entirely from the thoughts of the miracle but because the Galileans were coming back. It would not be long before he had his name.

19
ASCENSION DAY

It was the fortieth day since Jesus had risen, and Vinegar Boy worked in the hop fields with his sulfur pail and the small scoop. Sulfur protected the young plants from the hordes of tiny red spiders whose bite would sting the leaves and cause mildew or rot.

Behind him, Amoz, the overseer, was gently training the tendrils of the rapidly growing plants to climb the poles and trail across the interlacing ropes overhead. The vines must grow right, or the crop of cones in late summer would not hang correctly on the vines.

Above the boy the green terraces ascended the hill and ended at the low stone wall that separated the fields from the Bethany road.

A small bird swooped under the ropes and, like a runaway shadow, flitted beneath the vines. The whistling wings passed close to old Amoz and then brushed past the boy. The sparrow settled in a young mustard bush at the edge of the field.

As the little bird broke into melody, the boy heard

him. He set the pail of sulfur between the rows and stepped from the shade. The light breeze had thrown a dusting of the golden sulfur upon his hands and legs, and bits of brownish gold in his hair matched the happy sparks in his amber eyes.

In a few more weeks the entire hop field would be a sea of silvery green and yellow cones.

Many things could ruin the hop harvest—a swarm of lice, a horde of red spiders, a chill night, a fall of hail. Once he had seen the vines ruined at the very last day. But he felt confident about this year's harvest; the pickers would fill their baskets with the cones. Then the hops would be spread on racks inside the drying ovens, which bad been rebuilt since the earthquake and the storm. After the cones were cooled, they would be pressed into bags and carted to the commissary.

Sometimes the pungent, bitter yellow powder, called lupulin, which was deposited under the bracts of the hop flower, would be collected for the physician at the garrison. He would roll the powder into pills that would help ease a soldier's sour stomach or aid a restless man in going to sleep.

Sparrow scolded and sang and waited impatiently in the mustard bush. "Why are you here?" the boy asked. "Why are you not gathering food for your little ones? You are a bad father, Sparrow."

The bird ruffled his tail feathers and sang. Then he soared from the bush upward, across the terraces to the stone wall.

From the wall he sang and chirped and scolded. Before rising and winging toward Bethany and back again, his melodies tangled in his throat.

Then Vinegar Boy knew. He should have known at once. Sparrow was telling him that Jesus was in Bethany. For a few days after Marconius's last note, he had spent half of his time watching the Bethany road. But little by little, he had become more absorbed in the work with the hops.

There were people on the road and, as he thought upon it, he knew he had been hearing them for some time.

Jesus had come back to see His friends in Judea! This is what Sparrow was saying: *Jesus is here! Jesus is here!*

He had come to tell His loved ones good-bye.

As Vinegar Boy thought of what Marconius had said in his note, he paused for a moment. He wished he had time to run into the city and get Nicolaus, but the steward had warned him not to waste time.

He began to run up the hill, stepping on the stones of the terrace. People were coming from Jerusalem, moving in across the fields and from among the flocks and the cabbage patches. There was an orderliness and a quietness about their coming that struck the boy. All about them was an air of restrained excitement held steady by something that might be called sorrow or worship.

The boy hesitated at the wall, trying to find a familiar face. The faces were all friendly, but there was no one he knew. He climbed over the wall and followed. Sparrow flew ahead.

He was going to see Jesus. And he *must*—he *must* get his miracle. But Marconius had said there were no reports of miracles.

A group of children ran past him. One boy jumped to the wall and ran along, balancing himself, while his brother, a bit younger, tried to follow. The smallest of the children was a girl with clear blue eyes and cheeks as pink as oleanders. She stumbled, and her older brother yelled for her to hurry or she would miss

Jesus. She began to cry, rubbing her chubby fists in her eyes.

"Come on, little girl," Vinegar Boy said. "Let them walk the wall. I will walk with you."

The younger brother tormented her. "Tamar's a crybaby. A crybaby."

Her lower lip trembled, but she smiled at Vinegar Boy. "Did you know Jesus? I used to be sick all the time. He made me well. Did He heal you too?"

Envy pricked inside him. "No, I haven't been sick."

"He's going away into heaven forever."

Vinegar Boy nodded. The brothers jumped from the wall and were waiting. Tamar turned to him again. "Good-bye," she said. "I have to go now." She ran ahead, where he watched her chattering with the others. Once, she looked back and smiled, the sun bright on her brown hair.

Sparrow had hidden himself among the leaves of a fig tree, but his song betrayed him. The boy thought of Sparrow and their love for each another. But he had never held Sparrow in his hand. He had wanted to, but Sparrow would not trust him.

Still, it wasn't necessary to hold something close in order to love it. These people hadn't seen Jesus for many days, but they loved Him. There was a spirit of love between Jesus and His friends as there was a communion between himself and Sparrow. The boy felt another lift of joy within him.

On ahead, a woman with red hair reminded him of Magdalene. But it wouldn't be Magdalene; she would come from Galilee with Him. All the disciples had been in Galilee. He hoped he would see Mary. How happy she must be since her Son was alive again.

Would she cry when He went back to heaven?

"Oh, who will bring me the lilies of the field? Who

will press the star flowers into my hands and tell me that they match my eyes?" Her words from the crucifixion day rang in his ears as his eyes fell on a cluster of twinkling blue in the fields beyond the wall. He vaulted the fence, the stones warm under his hands. He plucked the flowers. Perhaps this was the very kind Jesus had picked for her.

In the pasture below, the sheep drank from a quiet brook. The stems of the flowers were dry. If he could wet them and wrap them in some leaves, they would stay fresh. He cast a glance at the road. Perhaps he shouldn't linger, but he wanted fresh flowers for Mary.

He scurried to the brook and knelt to wet the leaves. He saw his face in the clean water above the white pebbles. His ugly cheek showed dark and stained, purplish red like the hop seeds that were fit only to be thrown away. No vines were grown from the seeds—only from the sprouts.

His birthmark was keeping Nicolaus from believing in Jesus.

Above him the blue sky blazed, and large, white clouds began to roll. The willows moved and the water rippled, destroying the image of his face. But something caused his throat to ache.

Sparrow swooped above him, scolding furiously.

Hurry! Hurry!

The urgency was clear. Vinegar Boy leaped the fence and ran. Over the brow of the hill, the roadway was empty. Then he saw the gathering of people on the small, grassy hillock in the field.

Jesus must be there.

The boy pushed through the crowd carefully so as not to crush the flowers. He didn't have time to find his friends, for Jesus stood in the midst of them, ready to speak. Vinegar Boy looked at Him and sighed.

Marconius was right. There were no scars on His face or forehead. His garments were shining white. Light played above His head, and the hair that had seemed dark on the cross in the rain held a thousand bronze-red rays.

Jesus lifted His hand. Silence fell. The sleeve of His robe fell back, and the boy gasped. The hand of Jesus held a scar. A small, ragged mark the shape and color of a ripe mulberry marred the wrist.

Jesus spoke, and His calm, triumphant, loving voice rang in the boy's heart from that hour forward.

"It was necessary for the Son of man to suffer and be raised from the dead, for in this were the Scriptures fulfilled. For such a purpose I came into the world.

"But now My time has come to return unto My Father which sent Me. I came to do His will. In this can ye do His will also, that ye believe in Me whom He has sent. I came as a Physician to the sick, a Counselor to the troubled. I wiped the tears of those who mourned, and eased the hearts of those who grieved. I gave My life a ransom for many. It is not My Father's will that any who come to Me shall be turned away.

"Beloved, it is expedient that I return unto My Father, but I will not let you remain comfortless. The Comforter, which I shall send, shall abide with each of you. Tarry in Jerusalem until the power is sent. Thenceforth will the Spirit remind you of all the things which I have spoken.

"I say unto you, love one another. Serve one another, for in this will you show forth that ye are My disciples. Rest in Me, for your labors are ended. I am thy Sabbath and thy salvation. All power is given unto Me in earth and in heaven. I was in the beginning and shall be forevermore.

"Go ye, therefore, into every nation and preach the gospel according to the words which I have given thee. I go unto My Father, but I will come again. I am He that liveth, and was dead, and, behold, I am alive forevermore, and shall be with you always, even unto the end of the world."

As Jesus finished speaking, and while His hand was high in blessing, a dazzling light appeared out of the brightness about Him.

Clouds of purest white billowed and rolled beneath His bare feet. Above His head, trumpets sounded. The portals of heaven opened. Earth filled with humming, and those who had come to see Him dropped on their knees in the grass. Only a few kept their eyes fixed on the ascending Lord. And the boy heard the soft cry of a woman close at hand. "The angels! The angels from the tomb!"

He raised his eyes to see two men in white standing, one on either side of the hill.

"Ye men of Galilee, why stand ye gazing upward? This same Jesus, which is taken up from you into heaven, shall so come in like manner as you have seen Him go."

The brightness faded from the hill and large, white clouds overflowed the bowl of the sky, The murmuring of the multitude was like the wine of joy and the wine of mourning mingling in the same cup.

The crowd dispersed slowly. Vinegar Boy lingered, the leaves about the blue flowers drying in his hand. He climbed to the top of the hill where Jesus had stood and saw that the grass was still bent where His feet had last touched the earth. The boy put his hand against the grass and felt a living warmth.

What should he do with the flowers? The one woman who had called out about the men in white could have been Magdalene. Surely if John had been there they would have seen each another, but no one had seemed aware of anyone except Jesus.

On the road, the crowd had strung out so that only two or three walked together. At a Roman milepost, a young man waited. Vinegar Boy's heart leaped. It looked like John Mark. It *was* Mark—the boy who had been on the hill during the crucifixion.

Mark hailed him with a grin. "I thought it was you. I waited to thank you for your kindness on the hill that day."

Mark's young beard had grown darker and stiffer, but his eyes, shining gray with the rim of black, were as warm as Vinegar Boy had known they could be.

"Was John the fisherman here to see Jesus go?" he asked.

Mark nodded. "They were all here."

"Is Jesus ever coming back?"

"He said so, didn't He? We will have to wait. Until He does, He is sending the Holy Spirit to be with us. When the Spirit comes, Peter says we will be able to turn Jerusalem on its ear with our preaching."

"Who is Peter?" The boy had wanted to know for a long time.

"He is a fisherman, the same as John. Jesus intended for him to be a leader among us, but he turned coward. On the night the Temple guards and the mob arrested Jesus, Peter stood outside Pilate's porch and lied. He declared he was not a friend of the Galilean. It is said that he even cursed about it. Later he repented and wept bitterly. He was one of the first of the men to see the empty tomb."

Mark's voice grew a little proud. "No one will ever have a chance to say that I failed Him." Then he flushed and laughed. "Go ahead, tell me I am boasting. When I say things like that to Mother, she says I am like a loaf that is rising too swiftly."

"Did Jesus forgive Peter?"

"Of course! Jesus knew it would happen. You see, Peter needed a lesson. Nothing will ever make him deny Jesus again. He's going to be as solid as stone. His real name is Simon, but Jesus called him Peter, which means 'a rock.'"

"John told me. He said Jesus thinks names are important."

"Yes, I suppose so."

"I never had a name." It was easy to talk to Mark. "I was supposed to pick one after Jesus healed my face. I thought He'd be in the Temple that day, the same as always. It doesn't bother me as much anymore, but I have to pick a name so Nicolaus will quit worrying about me."

"What's hard about a name? There are hundreds of them."

Vinegar Boy shook his head. "It has to be the right one. But I know which one I want now. Do you think John would care if I borrowed his name?"

Mark laughed. "Why borrow when you can have half of mine for nothing? Nobody calls me John except Mother. She would be glad to know that another boy actually *wanted* it."

Vinegar Boy looked at Mark. The gray eyes were smiling warm and bright, and he felt the answering smile leap to his own face. Mark was giving him his name!

"Do you really mean it? You don't mind my having your name?"

"I would be honored," Mark said in a very solemn, old-man way, and both boys burst into laughter.

Later, as they walked side by side toward Jerusalem, Vinegar Boy said, "What does the name John mean? Do you know?"

"Well, Mother always said it meant God was good because He gave her a son. But I never thought it suited me. It's a little too gentle or something."

Vinegar Boy's heart leaped. Nicolaus would like the name, for he had often said the boy had come to him as a gift from the gods.

"I picked the flowers for Mary. Will you see her?" He had almost forgotten the little blossoms, and when he held them out, they were slightly wilted. The blue had lost its twinkle, and some of the sulfur from his clothes had speckled the green leaves.

But Mark smiled. "I will give them to her, and I'll tell John that you have a name. And I'll tell Peter that you and Nicolaus will be at the Temple to hear his first big sermon after Jesus sends the power of the Holy Spirit upon us."

Vinegar Boy laughed. "We'll be there."

They parted inside the city gates. A fleet shadow sailed past the boy and headed toward the nest in the eaves. A long worm trailed from Sparrow's beak.

In all the homes where the believers lived the business of the evening meal went on as usual. Already there were some who waited and watched for the Lord's return, not knowing that with God a thousand years could be as a single day.

20
ADOPTION DAY

Marconius didn't reach Bethany in time to see Jesus exalted. He rode into the barracks at sundown with the white mare in a lather. His boots clumped heavily across the threshold as he called for Nicolaus and the boy. Dust fell from the folds of his cloak. His cheeks were shadowed with beard and weariness, and he looked thin.

As he sat at their table, Vinegar Boy loosened his bootlaces, and Nicolaus set a bowl of freshly stewed figs before him.

Marconius listened as the boy told him of the ascension. The small, brown hands lifted as he told how the clouds swept under the Nazarene's feet and raised Him up toward golden gates that opened behind the billowing, white clouds. And he related eagerly the claims of the men in gleaming white robes who had told the people that Jesus would come again.

"He promised never to forsake us. How can He be

in heaven with Dysmas and down here with each one of us too?" Vinegar Boy asked.

"I don't know," Marconius replied. "But He knows. He knows everything: each time a sparrow falls, even the number of hairs on our heads."

The boy laughed and ran his hand over Nicolaus's bald head. "That would not be difficult with Nicolaus."

Nicolaus chuckled and asked the centurion where he had been learning so much about the Hebrews' God.

"I talked to many in Galilee. I don't intend to quit inquiring about Him. Such knowledge is like an empire of unspeakable riches. I'll never be like the mighty Alexander, who had to weep because there were no more worlds to conquer."

"But you are not a Jew, Marconius. I have understood that Jehovah is a jealous God, reserving salvation for the Jews."

The centurion leaned back and stretched. There were dust marks on the table where his arms had lain. The lamps were lit, and the dark eyes under the straight, dusty brows glowed with clean fire.

"There will come a time when I will sup at their table. They cannot count me unclean forever. Jesus is the Master of the feast, and He has invited me to come."

"There will be a 'day of adoption' for you, is that it?" Nicolaus said softly. "It could be. For such a time has arrived for the boy and me. We have been waiting for your return."

"You have picked a name at last?"

The boy smiled. "I am to be called John, son of Nicolaus."

Marconius nodded. "For John the fisherman? You have chosen well. That disciple is known as the one whom Jesus loved."

"You will see to the preliminaries for us as quickly as possible?" Nicolaus asked.

Marconius promised.

He brought word the next day that two weeks hence they were to see the judge.

The night before the adoption, Vinegar Boy was too excited to sleep. He called Sparrow from the eaves and talked to him as the moon rode like a white-sailed galley over the towers of the fortress.

He talked to Sparrow about his desire to be an honorable son. Putting his hand to his dark cheek, he said, "Someday I will have two good cheeks. Dysmas loved the sun, and Jesus took him to live where the suns are born. I will have a good face when it is time to have it. I think Jesus would like me to have Nicolaus believe in Him before He heals me. We will not worry about it anymore, will we?"

The sparrow bobbed its head sleepily, and tears warmed the boy's eyes. This was the last time he would ever cry about his ugly cheek.

Sparrow fell asleep on the window ledge with his head against his wing. Vinegar Boy reached out a finger and touched the soft feathers of brown and black. Sparrow moved uneasily under the touch as if the silver of the moonlight had grown heavy on his back.

The boy smiled as he said, "I would not harm you, Sparrow. Why do you not trust yourself to me? We are friends, you and I, and I wish you only good."

The bird slept on while the moonlight made a blanket for the sleeping boy.

Adoption day dawned clear and bright. Nicolaus spent the morning preparing himself and the boy with bathing and dressing.

Marconius came from his officer's quarters in full regalia. A scarlet plume bobbed on a new silver helmet. Medals and medallions gleamed like small suns on his bronze breastplate. The lace eyelets of his boots had been hand-polished, and they twinkled like low-flying stars. His scarlet cloak, matching the plume, swung in folds, short at the sides but touching his heels when he stepped.

Nicolaus was stiff and uncomfortable in his new garment. Woven of fine linen, it was a soft shade of gray with a heavily embroidered girdle of pale blue silk. His new freedman's cap covered his bald head, but the hair fringing the cap was snowy white and soft. He had oiled himself and cleaned his nails. There was no smell of labor upon him, and for a little while he seemed like a stranger to the boy. But the feeling passed as he saw the way Nicolaus looked at him. And he began to laugh as the steward walked through the halls, because Nicolaus's new shoes squeaked like frightened mice.

The boy wore a simple garment of creamy white cotton with a border of brown and gold threads around the squared neck. His hair, red-brown and shining, hung to his shoulders. Across his forehead it was cut short and lay high above the straight, golden brown brows. He wore new shoes of softest leather— soft as the sparrow's feathers they seemed against his toes. He had tried to tell Nicolaus that he was wasting his money on such fine shoes, because they would be worthless in field or garden. So different they were from the boots that were laid away in the chest.

When the day was done, he would put the new shoes and the new garment with the boots. He would keep them, and when he was old he would open the chest and tell his children and his grandchildren about these days in Jerusalem. The one great day of sadness and the many days of gladness.

At least, he supposed he could have children and grandchildren. Most boys grew up to become fathers. This was the way of life—even for sparrows.

He would probably never use the fine garment again. Not unless Marconius got married. Neither he nor the steward had been unaware that more than a search for knowledge about the Nazarene had drawn the centurion into Galilee.

In the large marble hall of the magistrate's office, the three of them stood, the two a little embarrassed in their finery.

"John, son of Nicolaus," the judge intoned, and the boy felt his heart leap.

Nicolaus tried to hold the pen steady as he signed the papers. The boy signed his own name, proud that Nicolaus had taught him to write.

Marconius stood at attention until time to sign as a witness. He had verified all that Nicolaus had told the judge and had added his own testimony as to the character of the steward.

Vinegar Boy had been questioned too. Oh, yes! Yes! Nicolaus was a *good* father. He had taken care of him ever since he was a baby and the soldiers had found him in the hills. His parents had thrown him away because he was ugly, but Nicolaus loved him. He made him study and do his lessons. He taught him to choose good rather than evil. He had never beaten him or forced him to do slave labor.

He would have gone on and on, but the judge held up his hand. "Enough. Until now I had believed that the gods resided on Olympus. Enough."

The papers were signed and the signatures blotted with sand and shaken dry. Other papers were written by scribes, and they, in turn, were signed and blotted. Then the papers were sealed with a blob of wax, and the judge pressed the official seal of Rome upon the warm wax. One copy was given to Nicolaus, who folded it carefully inside the pouch pocket of the woven girdle.

Vinegar Boy held his copy almost reverently; the parchment was cool to his touch. The judge shook the steward's hand and congratulated him on a new son. He shook the boy's hand, too, and called him John. The judge's hand was soft and spongy, making the boy think of the fisherman's hand with its hard nest of calluses.

Marconius shook their hands, too, very officially, as if he were not their very best friend. His grip was hard and firm.

On the way back to the fortress, they stopped at an inn where only the finest people were served. Nicolaus ordered a pitcher of expensive wine, small hot loaves with tiny sausages, and a platter of apricots. But before they ate, he asked Marconius to ask his Lord's blessing on the new father-son relationship.

Marconius laid a hand across the table. "Why not make my Lord your Lord, Nicolaus? Surely His Spirit has been speaking to you."

The steward's face went pink, and his eyes filled. His hand grasped John's, and the boy was almost too happy to eat.

Another family was celebrating at a table near them. The girl was about the same age as John, with hair long and shining brown. Her eyes were big and dark, gentle as the eyes of a desert creature.

She leaned across the table to speak to him.

"Is it your birthday too?"

Vinegar Boy swallowed. "No. It is my adoption day."

The girl said, "Oh," in a funny little voice, and he saw her whispering to her mother. Was she talking about his face? He didn't think so. Maybe she didn't know what adoption meant because she had her own mother and father.

A moment later she left her table and came to him. In her hand she held a golden ball of fruit. The boy had never seen anything like it. "Here," she said. "My mother says this is for your adoption day."

At first he shook his head, too embarrassed to take the gift from her. He could feel his good cheek getting as hot and red as his bad cheek. Then Nicolaus leaned forward. "It is not polite to refuse to accept a gift given in kindness, son."

So he took it and thanked her, and she said, "My name is Debra."

And he said, "Mine is John."

And she went back to her table, but every now and then he looked up, and she would smile at him.

The new fruit was cool to his hand. Marconius showed him how to peel it so that the inside fell apart into sections shaped like new moons. The fruit was juicy and sweet and the best thing he had ever eaten. The juice ran down his elbows and spotted his new garment, but Nicolaus told him not to worry.

That evening, as he went up the stairs to his room, he stood on the bottom step and said very loudly, so that Phineas might hear, "Peaceful dreams, *Father*."

And Nicolaus, who knew all things that the boy thought and who was only an arm's length away, answered in a roar that shook the walls, "The same to you, *My son*."

The next day in the hop fields, John spent the morning weeding and pruning. The weeds grew quickly, almost as quickly as the young hop vines. But nothing grew as fast as the hops. There were people who were willing to swear that the young plants grew more than the length of a man's hand in a single night.

And it could be so, for the vines fairly covered the rope arbor already. The blooms from the older vines made the fields a fragrant place.

The boy had been whistling, and Sparrow had been with him most of the day, hopping among the rows, watching for worms that clung to the weeds. He ate the worms himself now because his family had grown and left the nest.

Now and then, as Sparrow paused for an instant between the rows, the boy would attempt to touch him, but the bird would hop sideways or backward, casting a reproachful eye at him.

Then John would sing aloud to the bird. "I know a secret. A secret." And the sparrow tipped its head at him and looked up with inquisitive black eyes. "I know how your feathers feel. Soft as moonlight, soft as goose down, softer than the white lamb's wool. I know how your feathers feel."

Sparrow chirped angrily and dragged a resisting worm from a mass of roots.

Later, as the bird fluttered and chattered merrily, the boy said, "You are happy, too, little friend. But you rejoice because your family is gone, while Nicolaus and I are happy because we are a family."

The two of them left the hop fields in mid-afternoon. They came in past the grove of silvery green olive trees on the slopes of Gethsemane. Sparrow lifted himself on strong wings as the eastern gates came into view, and John began to whistle. He should be tired, but he wasn't. The sun had not burned him because the leaves of the hops covered the trellis. His heart was as full of happiness as the golden fruit had been full of juice.

He began to run and jump and was breathing fast and perspiring as he burst through the barracks gate and yelled, "Father."

Nicolaus came out at once, as if he had been waiting for him. He wore a clean apron and his face beamed. He was bursting with a secret. "Hurry, John. We have a guest."

When the boy stepped through the door and saw Mark, he wanted to hug him in joy. But he was beginning to think that he was too old to hug people, so he thrust out his hand.

Mark's face was shining the same as the steward's. They were both conspirators with a marvelous surprise. Mark's gray eyes were luminous as moons, and his beard had been trimmed and oiled just like a man's.

John looked at both of them and said, "What is it? What's the surprise?"

"Never mind," Nicolaus said. "We aren't going to tell you yet. You get cleaned up. We are going with Mark."

"Where?"

"Don't ask questions. Do as I say."

Mark laughed. "We can tell you this much. There is somebody who wants to see you."

"Who?"

"John, the fisherman."

Gladness almost closed the boy's throat. "He remembers me?"

"Of course he does. He has a gift for you too. So hurry up."

As he showered in the room where Nicolaus kept the buckets of water, he wondered what the fisherman could have for him. He washed and rinsed and then dashed, still dripping wet, through the corridor and up the steps to his room. He considered wearing the new garment but changed his mind. John would not care what he wore.

Maybe Mary would be there. Were they going to the village?

No, John must be in the city.

At the chest, he stopped. A small mound of grain was slowly rising on the lid. On the shelf above, Sparrow pecked away at the grain, which was pouring in a stream from the bag he had ripped with his bill.

"Sparrow! You're a thief!"

The bird chirped and looked guilty. As the boy pulled on his clothes, he said, "Do you know what the gift is, Sparrow? What the fisherman has for me?"

The bird sat still, his eyes fixed on the boy's face, And John laughed. "Aha, this is something that even you do not know. You have been too busy stealing the grain."

The bird remained silent. The boy rose from fastening his sandal strap and looked at him. Was Sparrow sick? Had he eaten too many worms, too much fancy grain?

Or was it possible that at last Sparrow was going to let him . . . no, it couldn't be. Not after all this time. Not Sparrow.

But he was. Slowly the small hand went out to the bird. Small fingers touched the softness of the warm, crouching breast. He felt the thumping of the excited heart. His hand slipped under the feet, and the tiny claws pricked. He lifted the sparrow. Sparrow's feet gripped his finger. John brought his other hand slowly and softly over the bird.

He held his friend in the hollow of his hand. Tenderness filled him as he felt the heart of Sparrow beating trustfully against him. Nothing could make him harm the bird. Was this the way fathers felt about their sons? Was this the way Nicolaus really felt about him?

"Hurry, son. Come on, John," Mark and Nicolaus called from the stairway. The boy set the bird on the window ledge. No matter what else this day held, this would be another day of gladness to add to the others.

He went down the stone steps three at a time, bursting out of the stairway before them. "Now tell me what the secret is," he demanded. "What does John have for me? If you don't tell me, I'll not go another step."

Mark threw up his hands and laughed. He looked at Nicolaus, and the steward beamed and nodded. The words came in a rush. "Peter and John are in the city. They are at the Temple. Peter is preaching and—"

Nicolaus could remain silent no longer. His arm drew his son near. His hand, hot with perspiration and emotion, passed slowly over the boy's dark cheek. "Peter and John are doing miracles, son."

The boy lifted amber eyes brighter than wine, clearer than sunlight. The happiness in his heart swelled until it broke loose on his tongue. "Father, oh, Father!"

He threw his arms about the steward. His own heart thumped against the heart of his father, as the heart of Sparrow had thumped in his hand. Jesus had known all the time. He had not forgotten.

And the boy knew just how it felt to be held in loving mercy in the hollow of his Friend's hand.

21
THE DAY OF
THE IMPOSSIBLE

Vinegar Boy pushed himself out of his father's arms and turned toward Mark with excitement. He could still feel his heart thumping and bumping as Sparrow's heart had thumped against his hand.

Happiness filled him. John, the fisherman, was back from Galilee. He was in Jerusalem. Mark had said so. He said that John and his friend Peter were doing miracles. Miracles!

Now he would get his face fixed. Jesus had not stayed long enough to do it, but John would do it.

But it still seemed too good to be true. He turned his amber eyes on Mark, who stood in the corridor of the commissary with his dark hair curling and a wide belt of fancy leather holding a fine green linen garment.

"Are they really doing miracles?"

This chapter is dedicated to Virgene Steffen's fourth grade class, Oak Street School, Orville, Ohio.

Mark laughed. "Cross my heart." He moved his hand across his chest to mark the X. "I saw them do one just a little while ago at the Temple near the Gate Beautiful."

Nicolaus's big hand closed gently on John's arm. "Listen, son, Mark has told me that the lame man who is always begging by the gate is walking now. Peter and John were there."

"Walking?" John's brow puckered. "He's been lame all his life."

"He's walking now," Mark said emphatically. "I saw it. Peter healed him."

"Peter?" A surge of disappointment ran through the boy. He didn't know Peter. John was the one who had said if he ever wanted a favor he should come to him.

Mark saw the flash of disappointment, and he laughed. "Does it make any difference who gives you a new cheek? If you want John to do it, he will. All of the disciples are doing miraculous things since the power of God has come upon them."

If Peter was doing miracles, then Jesus must have forgiven him for whatever he had done. Maybe He had Peter in mind when He said, "Father, forgive them; for they know not what they do."

What was it Nicodemus had said that day on the way to the hill? "You cannot rightly judge a day until the sun is set."

John had not fully understood what Nicodemus meant, but Nicolaus had explained. Nobody can say if a man is fully evil or fully good until he dies. Everyone did things that were wrong, things that were unwise, but they had other days in which to right the wrong, in which to grow wiser, in which to say, "I'm sorry."

"John," Nicolaus said, "Mark says that the man at

the gate wanted money but Peter and John had no money, and the beggar got angry. "

Mark laughed. "He banged his begging bowl on the steps so hard he broke it."

John grinned. "I guess if God knew Peter was going to do a miracle, He knew that the beggar wouldn't be needing it."

Nicolaus laughed, but John could see that Nicolaus *believed* Mark. The disciples *were* doing miracles! A look of wonder crossed his face—a shining look as of liquid gold, but the gold was lost beneath the dark shadow of the birthmark.

"Father, you really believe that they can do miracles just like Jesus?"

Nicolaus nodded.

Mark said, "Remember how Jesus spoke to us that day before He went back to heaven? Remember how He said we should stay here in Jerusalem until He sent the Holy Spirit?"

John remembered. He could still feel the coolness of the wet leaves around the violet-blue flowers he had picked for Mary.

He could remember the bright light and the warm grass. Jesus had told them that He had to leave them but that He would send a Comforter to be with them in His place.

Nicolaus and Marconius had talked about the Holy Spirit. The centurion thought that the Comforter could be described as Power. Nicolaus shook his head and said that the Comforter should be called Love.

Nicodemus, who came often to talk to Nicolaus and the boy, tried to explain it even more. Jesus could not be in all places at all times if He remained as a Man on earth. But the Holy Spirit *could* be in all places at all times. The Holy Spirit would dwell in the hearts of the people who believed that Jesus had died for them. But since the Spirit is a divine Personality they should speak of Him as a Person as they did of the Father and of the Son.

John had missed part of what Mark was saying to Nicolaus, but now he was listening, He was telling Nicolaus again about how the lame man had run and jumped through the Temple, praising God.

"And you think there is a miracle waiting for my son?" Nicolaus put his arm about John, and, as always, the boy could feel his father's love for him.

"Of course. There is nothing impossible with God."

"You really think they can get rid of my birthmark?" John put his hand to his cheek. He had learned to forget about it, but even so, he would be glad if it were gone.

"That shouldn't be half as hard as giving the beggar a set of good legs."

"Am I clean enough?"

"You just had a shower, didn't you?"

"Yes." Yes, he had run up the steps and found Sparrow stealing from the grain bag on the shelf. Sparrow? Where was he now? John wished that his friend could be with him when he got his miracle.

"What are we waiting for?" Mark asked, his black brows drawing into a make-believe scowl.

"For my father to get his freedman's cap. You know he wouldn't go anywhere without it."

Nicolaus came back, adjusting the cap on his head. It covered the bald spot, but the fringe of white curls showed.

"Father, should I change into my good shoes?"

"You look fine, John. Remember, clothes never make the man."

Mark laughed. "My mother is always telling me that, but to tell the truth, I like nice things."

Anyone could look at Mark and tell that he liked nice things. His belt was of expensive leather, and a small scrip, or purse, hung on his belt. His sandals matched the green of his tunic.

Nicolaus grunted in vague disapproval, but his blue eyes were smiling.

The moment they stepped out into the sunshine and started across the dusty bricks of the yard of the barracks, the boy's excitement grew. Now they went up steps past part of Pilate's porch. The guards recognized the steward and passed him on with a short salute.

Here there was a section of carpeted, mosaic balcony where Procula and Pontius Pilate could sit in the evening and get the breeze from the sea many miles to the west.

As they passed Pilate's quarters the boy glanced in. He remembered how he had raced through the halls trying to find Pilate and get an order for the aloes for Jesus.

Would Jesus remember?

Would Jesus let John have whatever power it took to give him a miracle? Maybe Peter would have to do it, but, to be honest, he knew he wanted his friend to do it. John was the kind of man he wanted to be, gentle and kind.

Long before they came to the strong iron steps that led down into the outer porch of the Temple they could hear the confusion of voices. John saw the sun dancing on the golden roof of the building. He could smell the smoke of the altar fire and the burning flesh of a sacrifice.

As they started to descend he wondered how they would ever find Peter and John in the crowd. People jostled people. They were talking, and arguing, and buying pigeons and doves. Some were haggling over the price of the grain and the oil for the offerings. Some were growling that the moneylenders had cheated them.

The boy wished Marconius had shown him the secret way that the soldiers used to get from the Fortress into the heart of the Temple area. But Marconius had never told him.

John stopped suddenly and turned to Mark. "Do you think we could find Marconius? If I get a miracle I want him to be there too."

"I'll try to find him. He must be here somewhere." Mark pointed. "I'll run down and find the disciples and tell them you are coming, and then I will find Marconius for you."

Mark started down the steps, two at time. "He'll kill himself," Nicolaus muttered, but John laughed. Mark, who wore the fancy clothes, was just like any other boy who loved to race down steps. John wished he could leap down, too, but he had to wait for Nicolaus. Why were old people so slow?

He felt a rush of shame and knew his birthmark must be glowing dark red. It didn't make any difference to him if Nicolaus took all day to get down. He would be glad to wait for him.

As they reached the first level of the steps, John leaned over. He could see Mark heading for a group of men near the gate.

Then John grabbed Nicolaus and pointed.

He had seen John the fisherman. He could tell even far away. And the bigger man must be Peter. The boy thought he saw a small bald spot on the top of his head, just like the one Nicolaus had.

Mark had reached John, and the boy saw the fisherman's head swing up. His eyes turned toward the stairs. Then his hand lifted. The boy's heart leaped, and he began to wave violently. He couldn't see John's blue eyes, but he knew they were shining with friendship.

"Come on, Nicolaus. Please hurry."

The steward went faster. He breathed harder. His feet hit the iron treads of the steps with solid thumps. And then Nicolaus stopped.

He was breathing hard, but it wasn't the exertion that caused him to halt. He laid his hand on the boy's shoulder and said, "Listen."

Peter's voice had lifted, and his words came clear. But for a moment Vinegar Boy did not think of Peter. The heaviness of his father's hand upon his shoulder made him think of Barabbas. Barabbas, and the darkness and the ugly odors of the alley. The alley was gone now, even as Barabbas was gone. The old tenement house had fallen during the earthquake on the day Jesus died.

"Ye men of Israel, why marvel ye at this . . . as though by our own power or holiness we had made this man to walk?"

Now Vinegar Boy saw the man who had been lame all his life. He was ragged, but he stood beside Peter showing everyone his good legs.

A silence began to fall over the people and priests in the court. The cries of the sellers and the moneylenders faded away.

Vinegar Boy thought God must have put His finger to His lips and whispered, "Hush."

Those who saw the beggar who had been healed began to listen to Peter.

"God . . . hath glorified his Son Jesus, whom ye delivered up, and denied him in the presence of Pilate, when he was determined to let him go."

John had spoken with poetry and tenderness on the crucifixion day, but Peter's voice thudded against the columns and the walls of the Temple like the hammer that had driven the spikes into the hands of Jesus.

"I know that through ignorance ye did it, as did also your rulers."

The priests and the elders who had clustered in anger began to mutter. *Who was this man to accuse them of ignorance? Was he not an ignorant fisherman from Galilee?*

Many of those who listened fell to their knees. Some cried and lifted their hands to heaven as if pleading. They had been among those who had cried for Jesus to be crucified. They had been among those on the hill who had mocked Him. Now they knew they had sinned against God and against His Son.

Vinegar Boy and Nicolaus watched as Peter and John walked among them, laying their hands on the bowed heads and speaking softly. Peter's voice had changed. He sounded more like John. "God, having raised up his Son Jesus, sent Him to bless you."

Now the Sadducees, who did not believe in a resurrection, began to agree with the priests and the elders and the Temple guards that something had to be done with these men before they convinced everyone to follow them and believe in Jesus. Perhaps they should arrest them. Scare them. Make them promise to quit preaching that Jesus could forgive sins.

For indeed, multitudes were crowding about Peter and praising God.

But Vinegar Boy saw John withdrawing from the crowd and coming down the stairs.

The boy waited on the second step. His heart was pounding as John reached out a hand to him. The big hand covered the little one, and Vinegar Boy remembered the nest of calluses on the fisherman's hand that came from rough work with the fishing nets and from holding the tiller during the storms on the Sea of Galilee.

No words came from either of them at first. Both were remembering the day of sadness. Then John spoke. His voice was as the boy had remembered it, flowing with richness as good wine. "How are you, boy?"

"Fine, sir. This is Nicolaus, my father." He spoke with pride, and Nicolaus smiled.

"He is my legal son now. His name is John, son of Nicolaus."

"I know." The fisherman was pleased. "Mark told me."

Vinegar Boy looked at John with serious, amber eyes. "I hope you don't mind. I really didn't take your name without asking. John Mark gave me the first part of his name because he didn't like it. I do. I want to be like him—and you."

The sunburned Galilean smiled. "I am flattered that you want to be like me. But, frankly, I would give all that I have to have a heart as pure as yours."

"He has always been a good boy," Nicolaus said and laid his hand on his son's shoulder.

"But goodness isn't enough, is it?" The boy looked up. Nicodemus had said something to Nicolaus about nobody being good enough. Everyone had done something that they were ashamed of, and only Jesus could forgive them.

"You must believe that He came to save you," John said softly.

"We do, don't we, Father?"

Nicolaus nodded.

"Somebody wants you," John said and pointed

toward the top of the steps. Marconius was there. Mark had found him. The centurion was in full dress. A red plume bobbed over a silver helmet. Bronze medallions blazed on his breastplate, just as they had blazed on the day of the adoption.

Behind Marconius and Mark the sun hit the stones of the fortress with red gold light. The light blinded the boy for a moment, and his vision was blurred. It seemed to him that the beam of light separated and crossed. He could see the soldier and his friend, and it looked as if they were on the hill again with the cross of Jesus behind them. He could hear Mark shouting, "This is Jesus of Nazareth, King of the Jews." He could see Marconius taking off his helmet and kneeling as he wept. "Truly this was the Son of God."

And then he seemed to hear another voice: *Whosoever shall give . . . a cup of water . . . in My name . . . shall not lose his reward.*

For a moment he was confused. Who had spoken? What cup of water? Nobody had given Jesus any water —only vinegar with a bitter drug in it. Now he remembered. John had told him.

And then before him, as though he were living it over in a moment's time, he saw the day of sadness: his flight to the hill; Barabbas under the stairs; the gourd of water from the fountain and the dirty loaf of bread. He saw Dysmas asking to face the sun, and he heard Mary crying. He could see himself picking flowers for her. He remembered the blisters and the cool grass and the storm, and he felt the smarting of the cheek where Nicolaus had slapped him because he was rude and sassy. But he had wanted the aloes for Jesus.

All of it, the whole awful day, went before his eyes, and he saw himself standing at the foot of the cross where Jesus was dying and saying, "Jesus. Lord. King."

And he felt again the push of the wind and heard again the crackling lightning as he clung to the cross begging in his heart for a miracle. "Now, Lord, please."

How long he stood gazing with blinded eyes into the sunlight beyond the centurion and Mark, Vinegar Boy never knew. But as it faded, he could see his friends descending toward him. The sunlight followed them. Little beams of light touched his cheek like warm fingers. He wondered if the fingers of sun had felt like this to Dysmas as they moved through his golden hair on the day he died.

He could feel the warmth on his dark cheek. Soft, the fingers were, soft as the silver moonlight that had warmed Sparrow's back on the night before the adoption. Something flew passed him, a soft shadow, a friendly chirp.

Sparrow was here!

The boy shivered with joy. All of his friends were here. Marconius, and Mark, and John, and Sparrow— and dear, dear Nicolaus, his father.

He didn't need anything else. He would never need anything else.

But he knew that he was to have something more. Because there was a love greater than his for his friends, greater than any man's friendship. Marconius had told him that Jesus had said His joy should be in them, pressed down and overflowing. Bushels and bushels of joy. This joy was running through him now, gurgling, laughing like a runaway brook.

Vinegar Boy turned. He expected John to lay his hand upon his cheek. To say something. But John didn't move. He didn't speak. Vinegar Boy saw that the fisherman couldn't speak because his blue eyes brimmed with tears.

Nicolaus thrust out his hand in an expression of

joy, and then, leaning over the iron balustrade, he began to weep.

Mark reached Nicolaus first and put his arm about the heavy shoulders. "I told you He could do it."

Marconius came nearer. "He's done it, boy. He's done it."

And then, strangely enough, the boy could hear the ecstatic song of the sparrow. He sat on the cornice of a white marble column, and he sang as he had sung on the morning of the resurrection day. Then he had sung, "He is risen. He is risen." Today the song was different. He was repeating what Marconius had said. "He's done it. He's done it."

The boy looked up at the centurion, light breaking across his face. Golden light that met no darkness.

"Marconius, is it really gone?"

The centurion's chin trembled; his voice broke. "It's gone, boy. Completely gone."

Vinegar Boy turned to John. The fisherman touched the unblemished cheek softly. "I had thought the gift might be through me, but God has His own mysterious ways of doing things."

Vinegar Boy threw his arms about the fisherman. "I will love you nonetheless. Now thank Him for me, will you? But tell Him I wish he had left just a little bit of it."

"Why?" Mark turned surprised and puzzled eyes on him.

Nicolaus waited for his son's answer. John was also waiting. Even Sparrow had stopped chirping and tipped his head to listen.

Vinegar Boy laughed, joy sparkling like wine in his amber eyes and across his fair cheeks. "Because," he said, as he reached for his father's hand, "it would help all of us to remember that nothing is impossible with God."

Also available from Moody...
...a dramatic audio edition CD based on the story of vinegar boy

---

To order your copy of this 55-minute drama call Moody Bible Institute's Cassette Ministries at 800/626-1224.

They are available to take your order from 9am-9pm Monday through Friday CST.

0-8024-6588-9, Paperback
Fiction/Youth (ages 10-12)

Moody Press, a ministry of the Moody Bible Institute,
is designed for education, evangelization, and edification.
If we may assist you in knowing more about Christ and
the Christian life, please write us without obligation:
Moody Press, c/o MLM, Chicago, Illinois 60610.